As soon as Chris Hamilton was out of sight, Felicity crossed her arms on her desk and buried her face in them, willing her heart to stop racing.

Had she managed to convince him that the letters were the unsettling but harmless result of someone with too much time on their hands? Because she'd certainly tried to convince herself. It had taken every ounce of self-control not to let him see that she was just as concerned as he was. She'd noticed his assessing gaze, looking for chinks in her emotional armor. As a reporter, she knew all about reading people's body language, too.

It had taken a lot of concentration to make sure her real feelings didn't show, and for some reason, with Officer Chris Hamilton sitting close enough for her to breathe in the warm, spicy scent of his cologne, it had taken more effort than usual.

* * *

DAVIS LANDING:
Nothing is stronger than a family's love

D0009417

Books by Kathryn Springer

Love Inspired

Tested by Fire #266
Her Christmas Wish #324
By Her Side #360

Steeple Hill Books

Front Porch Princess

KATHRYN SPRINGER

is a lifelong Wisconsin resident. Growing up in a "newspaper family," she spent long hours as a child plunking out stories on her mother's typewriter. She wrote her first "book" at the age of ten (which her mother still has!) and she hasn't stopped writing since then. Initially, her writing was a well-kept secret that only her family and a few close friends knew about. Now, with her books in print, the secret is out. Kathryn began writing inspirational romance because it allows her to combine her faith in God with her love of a happy ending.

KATHRYN SPRINGER
BY HER SIDE

Steeple
Hill®

Published by Steeple Hill Books™

ACKNOWLEDGMENTS:

Special thanks and acknowledgment are given to
Kathryn Springer for her contribution
to the DAVIS LANDING miniseries.

This book is warmly dedicated to Diane Dietz,
my editor at Steeple Hill, who understands the great mysteries of commas,
semicolons and ellipses, indulges my fascination (obsession?) with …'s
(most of the time) and who gently polishes my words until they shine.

STEEPLE HILL BOOKS

Steeple
Hill®

ISBN-13: 978-0-373-87386-9
ISBN-10:   0-373-87386-7

BY HER SIDE

www.SteepleHill.com

Printed in U.S.A.

Have I not commanded you? Be strong and courageous! Do not tremble or be dismayed, for the Lord your God is with you wherever you go.
—*Joshua* 1:9

The Hamiltons of Davis Landing

Nora McCarthy – m – Wallace Hamilton

Jeremy*	Timothy	Amy	Christopher (t)	Heather (t)	Melissa

*(son of Nora and Paul Anderson)

1. Heather's story: BUTTERFLY SUMMER by Arlene James   (LI #356, 7/06)
2. Chris's story: BY HER SIDE by Kathryn Springer   (LI #360, 8/06)
3. Amy's story: THE FAMILY MAN by Irene Hannon   (LI #364, 9/06)
4. Tim's story: THE HAMILTON HEIR by Valerie Hansen   (LI #368, 10/06)
5. Melissa's story: PRODIGAL DAUGHTER by Patricia Davids   (LI #372, 11/06)
6. Jeremy's story: CHRISTMAS HOMECOMING by Lenora Worth   (LI #376, 12/06)

Prologue

Ten Years Earlier

"Hamilton, maybe you should just throw a cot in the corner over there."

Chris Hamilton opened his eyes and saw his coach grinning at him.

"Are you leaving already?" he muttered, feeling his muscles tremble under the punishing weights he was balancing over his head.

He must have lost track of the hour. The last time he'd looked, three guys on the other side of the gym had been having a good-natured bench-press competition while the custodian mopped the floor. Now the lights were dimmed and someone had turned off the country and western music that had been blaring from the radio.

"*Already?*" One of Coach Swanson's ragged eyebrows kicked up a notch. "It's almost ten o'clock. And

I know for a fact that you have a big English test to-morrow first period."

Chris grimaced, but not from pain. The only reason Coach knew about the exam was because he happened to be married to Chris's English teacher. That was a bummer. He couldn't get away with anything. For all he knew, they traded notes about their students over their bran flakes every morning.

"I studied." Not that it would do much good. For some reason, when God had gifted the Hamilton family, He'd somehow overlooked Chris completely. Or maybe He'd just given Chris's twin, Heather, a double dose. Whatever had happened, he sweated over diagramming sentences more than he did bench-pressing three hundred pounds.

"Go home, Hamilton," Coach Swanson ordered, "and instead of dreaming about the next game, you better be conjugating verbs in your sleep."

Chris never ignored a direct order from his coach. He lowered the weighted bar into place and reached for the towel hanging over the end of the bench, swiping it across his face with one quick movement.

"Wish I had half your energy," Coach grumbled, then looked at Chris speculatively. "Had a talk with your old man the other day. He's pretty pumped up that you and Heather are graduating next month. Said he can't wait to get some more family members into the business."

Chris shrugged. "I guess so."

A familiar restlessness coursed through him. A

mixture of confusion and frustration that churned in his stomach the minute someone inquired about his future plans. Maybe it was because it usually wasn't an *inquiry* at all. People assumed that just because he was a Hamilton he'd naturally follow in his siblings' footsteps and stay in Davis Landing, becoming another efficient cog in the powerhouse that was Hamilton Media.

His dad, the incredible Wallace Hamilton, expected it, too. Instead of the usual bedtime stories most kids heard growing up, the stories Chris had been told were about the early Hamiltons and how they'd brought a small weekly newspaper through the Depression and World War II. When Wallace eventually took control, he'd turned the *Davis Landing Dispatch* into the successful media corporation it was now, which included not only the newspaper, now a daily, but also *Nashville Living* magazine.

So far his older brothers, Jeremy and Tim, and his sister, Amy, had already begun carving out their niches in the company. Even Heather was counting the days until she would be there full-time, planning to attend a local college and work at the magazine when she wasn't in class. Not him. The closer he got to graduation, the more pressure he felt. Pressure to take his rightful and expected place at Hamilton Media. The only trouble was, he had a sinking feeling there *wasn't* a place for him there. He had no desire to sit in an office and tally numbers all day and no one with an ounce of concern about the future of the company would want him writing for the *Dispatch* or *Nashville Living*.

Maybe that was why he was still in the school gym lifting weights instead of going home. The tension between him and Wallace had been escalating lately. Not a day went by that his dad didn't casually mention him "coming on board."

And not a day went by that everything inside Chris didn't tell him that Hamilton Media wasn't where he was supposed to be.

Maybe if he had a Plan B, something he could present to his parents, they'd be willing to listen. He knew his mom would. A lot of his friends complained about their moms. That they were overprotective. Worried too much. Not Nora Hamilton. She was a quiet but steady force in their family who'd taught her children that God had a unique plan for their lives.

So what was the unique plan for Chris Hamilton?

A heavy hand suddenly clamped onto his shoulder and Chris met Coach Swanson's knowing gaze. Had his coach seen a glimpse of the conflict raging inside him?

"Your dad will be proud of you no matter what you decide to do with your life," he said.

But Chris wasn't so sure. He turned down the coach's offer for a ride home and once outside, hit the sidewalk at an easy lope to work the kinks out of his muscles.

God, if You have something in mind for me, I hate to rush You, but You better move fast. Dad has his mind made up and I don't know how to tell him that I'd rather ask people if they want to upgrade their order of fries than balance accounts or write articles.

He took a shortcut through the back of the parking lot and that's when he heard it. A faint yelp. He eased his pace and then stopped when he heard it again. Only now he heard words. Shrill with fear.

"Just leave me alone! I have to get home."

"Did you hear that? He has to get home. Maybe his mommy will ground him if he's late."

Chris didn't hesitate. He followed the voices and when he stepped around the corner, two guys who looked to be in their late teens had backed a boy he recognized from study hall up against the building.

"Everybody knows kids from your side of town got money," Chris heard one of the guys growl. "Give it up or we'll have to beat it out of you."

"Two against one." Chris took a deep breath and stepped out of the shadows. "Doesn't look like a fair fight to me."

Not to mention that the kid pressed against the brick wall was a freshman and probably wouldn't tip the scale at a hundred pounds.

"Think you're going to even things up?" one of the guys sneered, lifting his fist. Which just happened to be wrapped around a baseball bat.

For a split second, fear skittered up Chris's spine. The boy they'd lined up as a target took advantage of the distraction Chris had offered and sidled up behind him.

What have you gotten yourself into, Hamilton? The thought raced through Chris's mind but he held his ground.

The guy with the bat took a menacing step closer. "This isn't your business, man."

"It is now," Chris said, forcing his voice to sound calm. Guys like this could probably smell fear. He had his doubts he was going to be able to talk his way out of this. Bat Boy didn't look like he'd be big on negotiations.

"Thanks, Chris." The boy hovering in his shadow barely breathed the words, but Chris heard him. For some reason, the quiet words gave him an unexpected dose of strength.

He was going to get them out of this. With both their limbs intact. He just wasn't sure how....

"Man, get out of here. There's a squad car," Bat Boy's friend suddenly hissed.

The glare of the headlights from a police car chased away the shadows and momentarily disoriented them. Chris's eyes adjusted quickly, just in time to see the guy with the bat pull it back in a broad arc. Chris guessed his intent immediately. To buy himself some more time to get away, he was going to let it fly at the two officers who'd jumped out of the squad car and were heading toward them.

Chris instinctively dove for the guy's legs, taking him out in a tackle that Coach Swanson would have been proud of.

"First down," he rasped at Bat Boy, who struggled to get away from him.

In less than five minutes, both the guys were hand-cuffed and sitting in the back of the squad car.

"Pretty quick reflexes." The cop, who looked to be

in his forties, looked at Chris and grinned. "Don't you think so, Jason?"

"Not bad at all," the other officer, Jason, agreed. Given the height and build of the younger officer, Chris knew Coach would've loved to recruit him as a linebacker for the football team.

"We've been having some trouble with kids being harassed lately and I have a feeling these might be our guys," the officer who'd complimented Chris said. "Could you boys come down to the station and give us a statement? We'll give you a lift home afterward."

A half hour later, Chris was in the break room listening to the officers' easy banter as shift change approached. Rich, the boy who'd almost been attacked, had finished writing his statement and his parents had already picked him up. Jason had taken the two guys to the jail for processing while Chris waited for Sergeant Evans, who'd made the arrest, to finish up some loose ends.

"The sergeant said you made a pretty gutsy move tonight," one of the officers said, sliding a can of soda over to Chris. "Handled yourself pretty well."

Chris shrugged at the unexpected praise and felt his face grow warm as the other officers shifted their attention to him. "I didn't have time to think about it."

"Ever think about our ride-along program?" Jason asked as he wandered in, tugging at the collar of his uniform.

"What's that?"

"High-school students interested in a career in law

enforcement ride along for a few shifts. See what it's like, whether it's a good fit. That's what sold me," Jason explained.

The officers laughed good-naturedly.

"You haven't made your probation yet, Welsh," one of them teased.

"Maybe he's recruiting his replacement."

Chris glanced at Jason but could tell that he was enjoying the attention. And didn't seem to take any of their comments seriously.

"Maybe I'm recruiting my future partner," Jason shot back.

Sergeant Evans appeared in the doorway. "Ready to go, Chris?"

Chris glanced at the clock on the wall and cringed. It was quarter after eleven. He should have called home the minute he'd gotten to the police department. Maybe by some stroke of luck everyone would be sleeping.

As Sergeant Evans pulled the squad car into the driveway a few minutes later and Chris saw a light glowing behind the curtains in the family room, he knew the chances of sneaking upstairs without disturbing anyone were slim. Hopefully it was his mom waiting up for him. Nora tended to listen first and ask questions later. His dad was just the opposite.

He opened the car door and Sergeant Evans pulled a business card out of his pocket and gave it to Chris.

"I'm sure you've got your future all figured out, but give me a call if you're interested in the ride-along program," he said.

Chris tucked it into his back pocket and paused to watch the squad car cruise away. Then he remembered the three chapters he should have had memorized by now. Sighing, he slipped in through the front door and stepped carefully around the floorboards near the coatrack that had a tendency to squeak. He'd been busted by that squeak on more than one occasion over the years.

"It's about time. If you didn't show up by midnight I was going to call the cops." Heather didn't even glance up from the textbook cradled in her lap as he tried to slink past the family room.

"That's who I was with."

Chris waited for her reaction and it didn't disappoint him. Heather lifted her nose out of the hallowed pages of the College Prep Advanced English text and her mouth dropped open.

"What are you talking about?"

He flopped into the chair across from her and gave her a play-by-play of the last few hours, ending with Sergeant Evans's invitation to take part in the ride-along program.

"You're going to, aren't you?" Heather ventured cautiously. "You *want* to. I can see it on your face."

Chris closed his eyes. How could he put it into words? He didn't quite understand what had happened, either. All he knew was for the first time in months, thinking about his future didn't give him that restless feeling. He felt excited instead.

"Come on, Chris," Heather urged quietly. "Talk to me. I know you've been having a hard time."

That shouldn't have surprised him. It was the weird bond between twins everyone liked to talk about. It was true, though. He'd always felt closer to Heather than he did to his older brothers. Womb-mates, she laughingly called them. Even though he and Heather were close, there were still some things she didn't understand. How could she? Everyone but him was a round Hamilton peg that fit into a round Hamilton hole.

"I did something that mattered tonight," Chris said. "And it felt good. Something bad might have happened to Rich if I hadn't stepped in. He was scared to death. So was I." He could admit it now but it hadn't stopped him from getting involved.

"But Dad…" Heather began, and then hesitated, not wanting to put a damper on his excitement.

She didn't have to. Chris had weathered his father's disapproval at various times over the years but even now he wasn't sure he could stand strong under the weight of his disappointment.

"Pray about it first, Chris," Heather said.

Her words hit him with the force of a pile driver. He had prayed about it.

If You have something in mind, God…You better move fast….

A sense of wonder washed over him. Maybe he'd already received the answer. Because even though he'd just spent the past hour with a group of police officers—people he'd never met until tonight—he'd felt like he fit in.

Chapter One

Present Day

"Time for the second shift to take over, Mrs. Hamilton. You're officially off duty." Chris slipped into the hospital room and wrapped one arm around his mom's slim shoulders, shoulders that felt too fragile to carry the weight that had been put on them recently.

Nora lifted her head and smiled at him. A genuine smile that momentarily eased the tired lines in her face. "Chris. I didn't think you'd be able to come by this evening."

"I talked to Jason and rescheduled my training. Thanks to all the times you've fed him supper, he owes me." Chris kept his voice low because he could tell his dad was asleep. "How has he been today?"

"The same." The words came out with a ragged sigh

and Nora's smile faded. "He did wake up a few hours ago, muttering orders."

Chris thought that might be a good sign. As weak as his dad was, he'd be more concerned if Wallace *wasn't* trying to run Hamilton Media from his private room at Community General Medical Center, where he'd been transferred recently following a bone marrow transplant in a Nashville hospital. Just when he was feeling well enough to be released, a low-grade fever had weakened him enough to keep him at Community General longer than they'd anticipated.

"I'll be here if he wakes up again," Chris promised softly. "Go home for a while, Mom."

Maybe a few hours of rest wouldn't completely erase the tiny creases that fanned out from the corners of his mother's eyes, but Chris figured it couldn't hurt, either. Nora had been incredibly strong during the past few months after Wallace was diagnosed with leukemia. Several rounds of chemotherapy hadn't been successful and finally Dr. Strickland, the oncologist in charge of Wallace's care, told them that only a bone marrow transplant could save him. Everyone in the family had been tested and none of them had been a match. Still, Nora had held up under the strain as the search began for another donor.

In a time span that convinced them of the power of prayer, a donor had been found and the transplant had taken place. Now it was just a matter of time—waiting to see if the transplant would be successful.

Nora's faith and encouragement had kept them all

going. The compact leather Bible she was holding in her lap was a permanent fixture in the room, giving them all strength and comfort when they needed it. But now...

It wasn't the bluish shadows under his mother's eyes that worried him. It was the shadows *in* her eyes. They'd appeared when Chris's older brother, Jeremy, had walked out on them and abruptly resigned from his position at Hamilton Media. Wallace had decided it was time to divulge a family secret and the bomb that he'd dropped—that Jeremy wasn't his biological son—had rocked the entire family. To make matters worse, in the midst of all the turmoil, his youngest sister, Melissa, had taken off for parts unknown with her boyfriend.

At a time when the tough fabric of family should have held them together, it probably felt to Nora, with her caring mother's heart, that they were being torn apart.

And he didn't know how to help her.

In fact, it seemed to Chris that he didn't know how to help anyone. Even using his contacts at the police department, he hadn't been able to find Melissa. And he certainly couldn't do anything to keep Hamilton Media going. Tim had stepped in and taken over as CEO while his sisters did their part to keep things running smoothly. All he could do was sit in the chair next to his dad's bed and make sure his mother remembered to eat and sleep.

As if she read his mind, Nora gave his hand a squeeze. "I don't know what I'd do without you."

Chris forced a smile and bent down to brush a kiss across her temple. "I'll call you in a few hours."

"I used to scold Melissa for calling you Officer Bossy, you know," Nora said, a faint glimmer of humor in her eyes. "Now I understand why she gave you the nickname."

Hearing his baby sister's name, frustration surged through him. Melissa must have known that her disappearance would only be another burden for Nora to carry. He'd done enough "search and rescue" missions with Melissa when she was floundering through her turbulent teens to last a lifetime. Not that he'd stop trying to find her now, even though she was an adult.

Maybe he didn't always feel like he had a lot in common with his family, but he'd give his life to protect them.

"If Vera Mae lets me in the kitchen, I'll make you and Jason a carrot cake," Nora said, returning the Bible to the nightstand. She knew he'd read it later.

"I'm not sure you can do that in your sleep."

"I can't sleep," Nora said simply. "But I do need to make some phone calls and take care of a few things at home."

When she stood up, Chris hugged her, wincing when he realized his suspicions were correct—she'd been wearing loose-fitting clothes so no one would notice she was losing weight.

"You can make us a carrot cake if you promise me you'll eat half of it," Chris whispered in her ear.

Nora chuckled. She knew she wasn't fooling him. "Maybe just a slice."

After she'd left, Chris took her place beside the bed.

He still hadn't gotten used to seeing his dad look so vulnerable. The chemo and the effects of the transplant had ravaged Wallace's lean, aristocratic features, leaving his skin pale and waxy. For Chris's entire life, his dad had been a force to be reckoned with. When he'd gathered his courage as a high-school senior and told him he was going into law enforcement, the silence that greeted his announcement was more deafening than if Wallace had yelled at him. He hadn't tried to change his mind, but Chris had felt an invisible wall between them ever since.

He'd take their awkward conversations any day over none at all.

"Get better, Dad," Chris murmured. "You can beat this."

Tammy Franklin, the floor nurse, peeked in and waved her clipboard at him. "I'm glad you convinced your mother to go home for a while. I've tried three different times today."

"Mom can be stubborn."

"Mmm." Tammy pretended to consider the statement. "I'll bet that trait doesn't run in the Hamilton family, does it?"

Chris grinned. Tammy could get away with teasing him because she'd been involved in Wallace's care from the beginning. His older sister, Amy, had told her once that they were going to make her an "honorary Hamilton."

"I'll be back soon to check his vitals. And I'll have a supper tray sent up to you."

Chris hadn't eaten since breakfast and his stomach rumbled in agreement. "Sounds great."

He leaned back in the chair and picked up the Bible his mom had put on the bedside table. A newspaper clipping fluttered out and he caught it before it reached the floor. He assumed it would be something from the latest issue of the *Dispatch* but instead he found himself staring at an article cut out of the *Observer*.

The *Dispatch*'s rival had somehow found out about Jeremy and printed the story, turning what should have been private family business into watercooler gossip. He glanced at the date and realized that the story he was holding was the gossip column that had printed the damaging news last month. A gossip section was a feature that Wallace had decided long ago the *Dispatch* didn't need to sell papers.

Why couldn't his father make those same faith-filled decisions when it came to his family?

The jumbled words he'd been blindly staring at came into focus. Just as he wondered why his mom had kept a copy of the column that the rest of them had delegated to the wastebasket, he saw the words she had written across the headline.

I sought the Lord, and He answered me; He delivered me from all my fears. Those who look to Him are radiant; their faces are never covered with shame.

Chris shook his head, a little in awe at the unwavering trust she had in God. She'd always told him and his siblings if they kept their focus on God, they'd never lose perspective. No matter what slander the *Observer* had printed, Nora had chosen to focus on what God's word said.

A soft moan from the bed drew Chris's attention and as he leaned closer, Wallace's eyes fluttered open. For a few seconds, his father stared at him with a blank expression that yanked at Chris's heart.

"Dad. It's Chris," he whispered.

To Chris's relief, his eyes cleared and recognition dawned in them.

"Where's…your brother?" Wallace rasped.

Chris swallowed hard against the sudden emotion that clogged his throat. Were things always going to be this way between them because he wasn't working at Hamilton Media?

"I'm right here, Dad." As if on cue, Tim had come into the room and was standing at Chris's shoulder. Silently Chris shifted out of the way so Tim could move closer to their father.

"How…are things going…at work?"

Chris couldn't help but notice the touch of arrogance in the smile that Tim directed down at Wallace.

"Everything's under control, Dad. Don't worry, just concentrate on getting better."

"Knew you could handle it," Wallace said faintly, his eyes closing again.

Just when Chris decided to leave them alone for a few minutes, Tim's hand gripped his arm.

"Meet me in the hall, okay? I need your advice."

Chris was too shocked to reply. When Tim strode out of the room a few minutes later, Chris was surprised to see that his brother actually looked worried.

"What's going on?"

"The past few weeks someone's been sending letters to the editor addressed to our new reporter. Unsigned, of course. The first one was a rambling complaint about the way she covered the last city council meeting. You know the type—they like to raise a fuss. Get some attention because they're anti-everything. The next one came and it didn't make much sense, either, but we printed them because it's our policy to give everyone a voice.

"When the secretary opened the mail yesterday, another one had come over the weekend. We're sure it's from the same person but this one didn't just attack her as a reporter, it was more personal. More threatening. I was hoping you could stop by the office tomorrow and talk to her."

Chris remembered Jeremy hiring a new reporter in May but he hadn't realized it was a woman. "Sure. I can come by around nine o'clock."

"Her name is Felicity Simmons. Don't be put off if she doesn't roll out the welcome mat for you. She doesn't want me to make a big deal out of all this but I'd still feel better if you read the letters and gave me your input."

Chris read between the lines. This wasn't Felicity Simmons's idea. It was Tim's. And Tim's will prevailed, as usual.

"I'll be there."

* * *

For the first time in the history of her career, Felicity Simmons was late for work.

She blamed her secret un-admirer. That's what she'd silently dubbed the person who'd been busy writing her letters recently.

When added to a restless night, a stoplight that had gone bonkers on her way to the *Dispatch,* confusing everyone who hadn't had their daily dose of java, *and* getting stuck behind a recycling truck that lumbered along in front of her like a mechanical brontosaurus, she would officially be three minutes late by the time she sat down at her desk.

"Hi, Felicity." Dawn Leroux gave her a friendly wave when she entered the building. She was standing near the reception counter, talking to Herman and Louise Gordon, Hamilton Media's elderly "gatekeepers." Even though they'd officially retired years ago, the couple were a permanent fixture at Hamilton Media. No one got past the lobby without an appointment— or their permission.

If she hadn't been running late, Felicity would have paused for a minute to say hello. Dawn wasn't only Tim Hamilton's personal assistant; the two women had met when Felicity began attending Northside Community Church shortly after moving to Davis Landing.

"Morning," Felicity called back, slightly out of breath from her dash across the parking lot. She made her way through the labyrinth of half walls to her "office" in the far corner of the room, the equivalent of journalistic Siberia. Farthest from the AP wire service and fax machine. And the break room. She'd accepted the cramped space with a smile, perfectly willing to pay her dues at the *Dispatch.* Not only was she the youngest full-time reporter that the daily had ever hired, she was also the first female.

If she didn't have a window or a desk barely bigger than her computer, so be it. She didn't expect any special treatment nor did she want it.

The telephone was already winking one red eye at her, letting her know she had some messages.

"Felicity, this is Tim. Push your nine o'clock appointment back to ten. My brother is coming to talk to you about the letter you got yesterday."

Felicity exhaled sharply. With Jeremy gone, the only brother Tim could possibly be referring to was Chris Hamilton. The police officer. She'd tried to play down her concern over the latest letter she'd received but obviously "Typhoon Tim" had taken matters into his own hands.

He'd gotten the nickname from the *Dispatch* employees and Felicity thought that it certainly fit. With some of the new changes Tim had implemented, she was surprised that half the staff hadn't jumped ship when he'd taken control.

Jeremy's leadership style had been as laid-back as his personality. The stress of a newspaper with its never-ending deadlines had the potential to tie everyone in knots but Jeremy had always been as calm as Sugar Tree Lake on a hot summer day. Tim was much more intense, which seemed to put everyone on edge. Still, she hadn't had a problem with him since Jeremy had left…

Until now.

She picked up the phone and tried to call Tim, hoping to change his mind. There was no response at his desk and she decided to track him down. Maybe he was on the second floor, terrorizing the employees who worked for *Nashville Living.*

Ducking down the hall, she headed toward the stairwell. Since the day she'd been hired, she'd been in a silent standoff with the ancient contraption most people referred to as the elevator. Fearless in most areas of her life, Felicity reluctantly called a draw when it came to enclosed spaces. She couldn't stand them. Besides that, the elevator was original to the building, which meant it had existed when people rode in buggies instead of cars. Another reason to opt for the stairs. And as well as *that,* exercise was good for a person….

Now, with every precious second counting, she paused at the elevator, tucking her lower lip between her teeth.

You're being silly, Felicity, she scolded herself. *You're a tough journalist, not a wimp. This is a three-storey building, not exactly a skyscraper.*

She decided that whomever promoted self-talk as a good way to motivate a person hadn't been afraid of small spaces. It was a good thing she knew what *did* work.

Lord, You promised to give courage to the faint-hearted. I'm taking You up on it! Please give me courage.

The elevator's low, musical beep sounded and before Felicity could move, the door swished open.

She was trapped.

Not by the elevator, but by the man stepping out of it. For a second, the only thing in her field of vision was the color blue. Then the badge came into focus. Felicity wasn't petite but the man who took a step forward seemed to tower above her. When she lifted her eyes to his face, she saw a familiar combination of features—the chiseled face, firm Hamilton jawline and a pair of warm, intelligent eyes that happened to be the same shade of brown as the caramels she had stashed in her desk drawer.

He stepped politely to the side and she could breathe again. Wait a second. Why was she holding her breath?

"Two or three?" he asked, holding the door for her.

"Neither." Felicity buried a sigh and extended her hand. "I'm Felicity Simmons and if you're Officer Hamilton, I believe we have an appointment."

Chapter Two

"My office is just down the hall in the newsroom. I have several appointments this morning but I adjusted my schedule."

Chris barely felt the warm press of Felicity Simmons's hand before she pivoted sharply and moved away, her low-heeled shoes clicking against the marble floor. He fell easily into step beside her.

"I have to be honest. I wish Tim wouldn't have bothered you. I can't help but feel like we're wasting your time," Felicity went on.

Chris didn't answer right away. He was still suffering from the mild case of shock he'd been hit with when Felicity had introduced herself. He'd taken a few minutes to go up to the second floor to say hello to Amy and Heather, who were hard at work on the next issue of *Nashville Living*. It had been Heather who'd told him where to find Felicity, but when the elevator door had opened and he saw the woman standing on the other side, his first assumption was that she worked in the accounting department.

She was younger than he expected. Probably close to his age. Even though she looked every inch the professional in conservative brown pants and a matching jacket, with her auburn hair swept away from her face and anchored in place by an industrial-strength copper clip, he never would have guessed she was F. Simmons, the reporter who had covered the last city council meeting. She'd written it with bold honesty, not attempting to soften the heated debate several councilmen had engaged in over some proposed budget cuts.

"History meets modern technology," Chris murmured as Felicity pushed open the swinging door between the front lobby and the part of the building that housed the *Dispatch*.

The historic beauty of Hamilton Media had bowed to progress when it came to the *Dispatch*. The original high tin ceiling was still in place but the room had been converted into a maze of half walls and computer stations. As they entered the newsroom, no one paid any attention to them as they weaved their way to Felicity's desk. Chris could sense the tension in the air and he was thankful he didn't have a deadline hanging over his head every day. Although he knew his mom would have preferred he face a deadline instead of the wrong end of a gun.

"Please sit down," Felicity said, her voice brisk as she slid into the narrow space behind her desk. She motioned for Chris to take the chair across from her.

"It isn't unusual for reporters to step on people's toes. Or to get letters from disgruntled citizens about an issue that ruffles their feathers."

"With all that's been going on lately, I'll have to admit I haven't read an issue of the *Dispatch* for the past few weeks."

Right before his eyes, the no-nonsense reporter changed. She suddenly seemed to see him as a person, not as a cop who was interrupting her schedule.

"I know this must be hard on your family." Her voice softened and it brushed against his defenses.

In the past few weeks he'd gotten used to people politely inquiring about Wallace and murmuring their surprise at the change in the hierarchy at Hamilton Media. Sometimes they asked questions that made Chris wonder if it wasn't simply idle curiosity motivating them, but he saw none of that now in Felicity's eyes.

Usually he was dead-on with his insight into a person's character from the moment he met them. Now he had to adjust his assessment of Felicity Simmons. She wasn't as tough as her brisk manner and business-like attire suggested.

We're doing all right. That's what he started to say. It had become his standard, by-the-book comment. Those words couldn't cover the sense of loss he'd felt when the family had gathered for their traditional monthly dinner not long ago. Not only had Wallace's chair at the head of the table been empty, but so were Melissa's and Jeremy's. They also couldn't begin to express the helplessness he felt when he watched his mom try to be strong for everyone. Or that he couldn't make everything right.

"One minute at a time. Trusting God is the only way we're getting through it." He surprised himself by telling her the truth.

"That's the only way we can get through anything," Felicity murmured.

Adjustment number two. She was a believer.

"I'd like to read the letters Tim told me about." Back to business. He needed to dwell on the reason he was here instead of the way Felicity's eyes met his in complete understanding. And the fact they were the color of sweet tea. "He mentioned the last one seemed more threatening."

Felicity nodded but the way she lowered her gaze for a moment raised a red flag.

"You didn't destroy it, did you?" Chris asked, more sharply than he intended. It wasn't unusual for women who were being stalked to delete threatening e-mails or burn letters, as if getting rid of the threats was comparable to getting rid of the person making them. Without the necessary evidence, an investigation came to a grinding halt.

Felicity shook her head. "I still have it."

She leaned over the desk and wordlessly handed him some tear sheets from the two letters they'd printed in the newspaper.

Chris read the first one, a rambling commentary about the *Dispatch* being biased in their coverage, but it was obviously directed at Felicity because the person who'd written it mentioned *her.* Felicity was the only female reporter on staff. The second one again mentioned an unfair bias and then ended with a veiled threat: You'd better stop before it's too late.

Chris paused and looked up at Felicity. Body language was an important part of the interview process and he noticed immediately that her hands were in a relaxed pose on top of her desk. She didn't have her arms crossed. She wasn't fiddling nervously with a pen or shuffling papers. She was patiently waiting for him to finish so she could get on with her day.

"What do you think they want you to stop?"

"I have no idea." Felicity met his gaze evenly. "Since May, I've been covering city council meetings and attending court hearings. I've done the lead stories for two different jury trials. One was the drunk driver that pushed a car full of teenagers into the river, the other was a special-interest piece on the mayor's vision to balance community development with economic development."

"Aren't they the same thing?"

"You wouldn't ask that if you'd been to the last council meeting." Felicity chuckled.

That dash of humor and the glint in her eyes told Chris that she enjoyed the challenge of her profession. He could appreciate that. So did he. Maybe his family didn't understand why he'd wanted to be a cop, but even on his worst day he wouldn't trade it for anything else.

Felicity pulled out a piece of paper and handed it

to him. Reluctantly, Chris thought. "This one was delivered over the weekend. Addressed directly to me, not
the newspaper."

Things are different here than where you're from.
If you keep it up, you'll find out that people take
care of their own problems in their own way. Just
a reminder to you to watch your step.

A veiled threat, but it sounded a little more serious
than the last one. Obviously the letter writer had some
knowledge of Felicity's background if he knew she
wasn't from Davis Landing. He'd subtly branded her an
outsider.

Chris stared at the letters, wishing he had more to
go on.

"Did the first ones come through by e-mail originally
or were they sent to the paper through the post office?"

"The post office."

Chris exhaled slowly. E-mail messages might have
given him a better lead. He could have traced the sender
to a specific e-mail account through the local server.
"Did you notice a postmark?"

"Local."

Chris was impressed that she'd thought to look. Obviously her attention to detail wasn't simply a charac-
teristic of her skill as a reporter.

For some reason that he didn't understand, Chris
was uncomfortable having to ask the next question. "Is

it possible this is someone you know? Someone you met socially? Maybe dated?"

Color tinted Felicity's cheeks. "The only people I've spent time with since I moved here attend Northside Community. I don't have time to socialize."

Now why did he have the urge to smile even though she was obviously upset with him now? "They're standard questions, Miss Simmons. I'm sure, being a reporter, you understand."

"Of course, and I'm sorry." Felicity's voice switched back to professional mode. "You're just doing your job and you've probably received threats, too. It just goes with the territory. I'm sure the letters are harmless— the neighborhood bully trying to intimidate the new kid on the block."

Chris wanted to reassure her. He admired Felicity for handling the situation so calmly, but to not be cautious and alert—to not take the letters seriously— wouldn't be the wisest course, either. Frustratingly enough, with the flimsy evidence, there wasn't much he could do from a legal standpoint. And he had the feeling she knew it, which was probably why she'd made the comment earlier about wasting his time.

"Let me know if you receive any more letters and be sure you document them." Chris found himself reciting the usual precautions and the words left a bitter taste in his mouth. "Have your answering machine record your phone calls. Be aware of your surroundings, especially at night or when you're alone. I'm sure your coworkers know about the letters, but let them know you'd appreciate it if they keep their eyes open for anything suspicious. Someone hanging around your car in the parking lot. Someone who calls the newspaper, asking questions about you, maybe looking for personal information."

Felicity had been nodding in agreement during the beginning of his list but suddenly her expression changed. "Do you think it's really necessary to mention it to my coworkers? I asked Tim to keep the last letter between the two of us. I don't want it to look like I'm being coddled. Other reporters have gotten hate mail in the past."

Seeing the determined tilt of her chin, Chris had the sudden urge to put her in lockup until he could figure out who their anonymous letter writer was. He had the uneasy feeling that Miss Felicity Simmons's confidence was going to get her into trouble.

"Let me ask you a question. Who has more wisdom—the person who walks down a dark path at night with their hands in their pockets, staring down at the ground, completely unaware of their surroundings, or the person who walks the same path but is alert? Not petrified, but cautious? Aware that there may be things out there they can't see?"

"All right. You won this round." Felicity sighed and then smiled at him.

She should be cited for carrying a concealed weapon, Chris thought, momentarily blown away by the transformation. The minute the elevator door had opened, he'd acknowledged the fact that Felicity was pretty, but that smile took her from serious to stunning.

Chris wondered if she knew it totally ruined the whole "tough reporter" persona. Especially when it coaxed the dimple that lurked near the corner of her lips out of hiding.

Unnerved, he rose to his feet. As his brain cells began to function again, he took a few steps, then paused and glanced over his shoulder.

Felicity was already sorting through some papers.

"Miss Simmons?" he prompted softly.

Felicity looked up.

"Just a reminder. I'm one of the good guys. I'm on *your* side."

As soon as he was out of sight, Felicity crossed her arms on her desk and buried her face in them, willing her heart to stop racing.

Had she managed to convince him that the letters were the unsettling but harmless result of someone with too much time on their hands? Because she'd certainly tried to convince herself. It had taken every ounce of self-control not to let him see that she was just as concerned as he was. She'd noticed his assessing gaze, looking for chinks in her emotional armor. As a reporter, she knew all about reading people's body language, too. He wanted to see if she was telling the truth—did she maintain eye contact or did she look away from him? Was her posture open or closed?

It had taken a lot of concentration to make sure her real feelings didn't show and for some reason, with Officer Chris Hamilton sitting close enough for her to breathe in the warm, spicy scent of his cologne, it had taken more effort than usual.

"This is all I need," she murmured. "Just when Lyle and Glenn are starting to accept me, I end up in the crosshairs of some lunatic who doesn't like the way I report the news."

Lyle Kimble and Glenn Rhodes were the other full-time reporters. They were both in their late forties, had started as stringers and built their reputations over the years by printing the truth, setting peoples' teeth on edge and earning the respect of their readers one issue at a time.

Felicity had a degree in journalism with a minor in political science, six years working at a weekly newspaper in her hometown, supportive parents and sheer determination.

After weeks of feeling the temperature in the newsroom drop when she walked in, the first letter to the editor Felicity received had actually started the equivalent of a spring thaw. Lyle had laughed and Glenn had given her a friendly clip on the shoulder after he'd read it.

"This is your rite of passage, Simmons. The first person you ticked off enough to write to the editor. Frame it."

She hadn't framed it. Instead of a rite of passage, it was evidence. Chris had taken the tear sheets with him when he left and they were probably already in a file at the D.L.P.D. with her name on it.

Chris. Remembering his last words made her smile again. Now that she thought about it, when he'd told her to keep the other *Dispatch* employees updated on the situation, she *had* sounded a little argumentative. As if they were squaring off in opposite corners of a boxing ring.

Her gaze shifted to the porcelain frame propped on a small gold easel near the corner of her desk. It was one of the first things she'd unpacked when she'd arrived at the *Dispatch*. Her mom had copied one of her favorite verses and given it to her as a going-away gift before she'd moved to Tennessee.

Have I not commanded you? Be strong and coura-geous! Do not tremble or be dismayed, for the Lord your God is with you wherever you go.

It was a promise Felicity had clung to over the years. As a high-school sophomore, when she'd attended a Washington D.C. young journalist's conference. When she'd left for college. When Jeremy had hired her to work at the *Dispatch*.

And after she'd received the threatening letters.

God was with her. He'd protect her. Like Chris had said, one minute at a time. Trusting Him.

Chris. A little dismayed that her thoughts had re-turned to him, Felicity tried to replace him by skimming an article on her desk. After reading the same sentence three times, she gave up. He stubbornly remained in her memory. Typical of a Hamilton, she thought wryly. They did have a tendency to make an impression.

It was strange that she hadn't seen him around Hamilton Media before. Nora dropped by on a regular basis to say hello but Felicity had never seen Chris. She didn't see him on Sunday mornings at Northside

Community Church, either, where the rest of the Hamilton family worshipped. From the simple statement he'd made about trusting God, it was clear that he was a believer, but maybe his shift only allowed him time to attend the Sunday evening services that Northside Community offered.

She frowned, tracing her pen along the margin of the article. It wasn't unusual for her to see the officers at circuit court. Maybe she'd caught a glimpse of him there at some point and hadn't realized who he was.

Right. Like you would have forgotten him!

Felicity shook the pesky thought away. She was focused on her career and so far nothing—or no one— had distracted her. Hopefully now that he'd interviewed her, Chris would set Tim's mind at ease that there wasn't anything the police could do about the letters and she could continue to report the news. And she and this particular officer—all right, this particular *attractive* officer—wouldn't be crossing paths again.

Chapter Three

Chris didn't make it to the revolving door at the front entrance of Hamilton Media before Tim intercepted him.

"What's the verdict?"

Chris plowed his fingers through his hair. "Anonymous stalker. Angry. Intelligent." *A bad combination.* "My guess is that he's familiar enough with the legal system to know that if I knocked on his door and hauled him in right now, he'd be out in time to have lunch at Betty's Bakeshoppe. His threats are subtle but definitely escalating. At this point, he's trying to scare her."

And it wasn't working.

Remembering Felicity's calm response to the situation rekindled the respect he'd had for her during the interview.

"So it's nothing to worry about. He'll lose interest."

"I wouldn't say that. I know we don't have much to go on, but I'd like to do some follow-up anyway."

"Tell me this isn't going to mean more bad publicity for the company."

Tim's comment made Chris's back teeth grind together. "Is that what this interview was about? Protecting the *company?*"

Tim's eyes held no apology. "Of course I'm concerned about Felicity, but you know as well as I do that when the *Observer* printed the story about Jeremy a few weeks ago, it was sending a message. Anything that happens at Hamilton Media—and to our family—is fair game. It's news. And I refuse to become fodder for the *Observer*'s gossip column."

Chris wasn't exactly thrilled by the possibility either but in his mind, Felicity's safety outweighed the cost of negative publicity.

"Felicity isn't taking this very seriously, either. Someone has to." Someone had to protect her.

"I'll talk to Dad," Tim said, as if that settled it.

Chris sent up a silent prayer for patience. "This isn't Dad's decision," he pointed out. "You asked me to talk to Felicity as a police officer. I'm on *duty.* I write a report, file it and then I decide the best way to go from here."

They hadn't had a stare-down contest since they were kids, when they needed something to kill time on long car rides or while they waited for dinner. When he'd gone up against Jeremy, Jeremy was always the hands-down champion but it could go either way between Tim and himself.

This time he won. So he was twenty-seven years old. It still felt good.

Tim smiled faintly. "Whatever you think is best, *Officer Hamilton*. I wouldn't want you to arrest me for—"

"Obstruction," Chris said helpfully.

"Right." Tim gave him a mocking salute but there was a glint of laughter in his eyes. "I better get back to work. One of us has to keep Hamilton Media at the top."

Chris knew it wasn't a deliberate cut but he still felt the sting. He knew that Tim would discuss the situation with their father but for once Wallace wouldn't have the final say. Felicity's stalker wasn't just Hamilton Media business anymore. It was police business. And, depending on Chris's decision, another wedge that had the potential to drive him and his dad further apart.

"You're still here? Did someone do something about the funky traffic lights at the corner yet?" Felicity swept past him and was several yards away before he realized she'd asked him a question.

He caught up to her in two easy strides.

"Where are you off to, Lois?"

She didn't miss a beat. "There's a guy in blue tights I have to interview. Kind of strange if you ask me. Spandex isn't the most comfortable fabric."

"I'll take your word for that." Chris grinned.

Felicity headed toward the parking lot, skirted around the police car and slanted a look at him when he remained at her side. "Is this a police escort, Officer Hamilton?"

"Just walking a lady to her car." *Power walking a lady to her car.* In spite of the oppressive August heat, Felicity moved in fifth gear. And not a hair out of place, either.

"It's broad daylight," Felicity said, with just a touch of exasperation. "I'm sure I'll be…"

She stopped so abruptly that Chris slammed into her. The momentum pushed Felicity forward and instinctively Chris reached out to steady her. His hands wrapped around her arms and she winced.

"Okay, maybe I should be interviewing you instead of the guy in the blue tights. Maybe *you're* the super-hero."

"Sorry. My Kevlar vest." Chris's lips twitched. "And I hate to disappoint you, but I'm only bulletproof when I'm wearing it."

"This is why I don't wear heels," Felicity grumbled as she pulled off one leather shoe and inspected it.

"So that's why you stopped. You have a *flat.*"

Felicity twisted around to face him and the movement brought her into close range. So close he could see that her velvety brown irises were ringed with copper.

"No, I stopped because of *that.*"

Chris followed the direction she was pointing and his gaze settled on a baby-blue Cadillac straight off the set of *Happy Days.*

He would have whistled his appreciation except for one thing. Both back tires had been slashed.

* * *

Felicity pushed her shoe back on and headed over to survey the damage. Anger surged up and crested inside her. She dug into the pocket of her linen blazer for a caramel candy. Popping it into her mouth, she looked from the tires to Chris, who was prowling around the car. The humor had vanished from his eyes and his mouth had flattened into a grim line. He looked every inch the police officer.

"Don't kids have anything better to do than vandalize people's property?" And here she'd been harping about nothing happening in a parking lot in the middle of the morning.

Her words pulled at Chris's attention. "You're sure this was kids?"

In an instant she knew what he meant. Her secret un-admirer. She refused to believe it.

"It had to be." The words sounded weak, even to her. She scanned the nearest vehicles parked close to hers, searching for similar damage. No. Just her beloved Caddy.

"What time did you get to work this morning?"

"About quarter after eight."

"Do you park in the same place every day?"

"I park wherever I can find a spot." Which meant that if it was her un-admirer, he knew what kind of car she drove. A cold shiver danced up her spine, raising the hair on her arms.

She could see by Chris's expression that he had come to the same conclusion.

"I'll call a tow truck." He lifted his radio out of the

holder on his belt and took a few steps away, murmuring quietly into it.

Felicity looked at her watch and resisted the urge to howl. But then Chris would have felt obligated to make another call for someone to come and take *her* away. She concentrated on the caramel candy that was melting in her mouth even though what she *really* wanted to do was crush it between her teeth. Her dad's anti-stress remedy. He'd told her by the time the candy had dissolved, so would her temper. And it always worked. Well, most of the time. She'd kept a pocketful since she was seven years old.

"All set." The frown that had settled between Chris's eyebrows was still there. "They're on their way."

"This guy didn't happen to leave a message under my windshield wiper, did he? Maybe one with a letterhead on it?" Felicity tried to ease the tension with humor. She couldn't let him see how the mangled tires had affected her equilibrium. She propped one hip against the door to steady herself. Her legs felt like overcooked pasta.

"He left a message all right." Chris bumped the shredded tire with the toe of his boot. "It's right here."

"Felicity told me about her tires." Tim showed up at the police department later that afternoon. "Someone's car was keyed in that parking lot a few weeks ago."

Chris's breath hissed between his teeth. "Usually if it's vandalism, someone sticks a knife in the tire and walks away. The air seeps out, the tire goes flat.

The vandal walks away. Felicity's tires looked like fettuccini. There was a truckload of aggression driving that knife into the rubber."

"Dad doesn't want any more publicity."

"I'm going to follow up on this." Tim valued the direct approach, so Chris was going to be direct. "And I'm off duty in a few minutes. Let's go talk to Dad together."

Hopefully they could put aside their differences to make the best decision. For the family *and* Felicity.

There was no way he was going to step away from this now. No matter how Felicity had kept up a show of bravery, he still had a hunch it was all show. Letters were easier to ignore than a blatant attack on your personal property. When the mechanic had loaded up the car, Felicity had given the convertible a final comforting pat on its baby-blue fin. And for a split second, he'd seen the flicker of fear in her eyes.

"We can take my car to the hospital," Tim said.

The Ferrari. Okay, he was big enough to admit it. He practically drooled with envy whenever he saw his brother's mode of transportation but he wasn't going to pass up an opportunity to enjoy those butter-soft leather seats and the low purr of an eight cylinder, either. He'd leave his motorcycle baking in the parking lot for a few more hours.

"Can I drive?"

Tim's bark of laughter echoed around the room and Chris realized that laughter had been something their family hadn't indulged in much lately. Especially Tim. He was so much like Wallace—so confident and driven—it was easy to assume he'd taken his place at the company helm without any additional effort. Now, Chris suddenly wondered if that was true.

"No way. I'm not giving my keys to someone who took out a mailbox the day after he got his learner's permit." Tim tossed the keys in the air and deftly caught them again.

"You really need to learn to let go of things, bro."

When they got to the hospital, Nora and Heather met them in the hallway. Heather walked right into his arms without hesitation. Her cheek rested against his shoulder and he patted her back, feeling the tremors that coursed through her.

"Nice to know that you still need your brother now that you've got Ethan hanging around," Chris whispered teasingly, referring to *Nashville Living*'s staff photographer—and the reason Heather was walking two feet above the ground these days.

Heather's fingers wiggled into his ribs and he jumped. She'd discovered his weakness when they were four and never let him forget it. "I'll always need my brothers," she said, then lowered her voice. "*All* of them."

Jeremy. A silent message passed between them. Although Jeremy still spoke with him on the phone occasionally, Chris was getting concerned about what he saw as Jeremy's increasing detachment from the family. At first he'd thought his oldest brother just needed some time and space but lately Jeremy seemed to be pulling away from them even more.

Chris kept one arm around Heather and wrapped the other one around his mother, bending down slightly to plant a kiss on her temple.

"We were just going to the cafeteria for something to eat," Nora told him. "Do you and Tim want to join us?"

"No." Tim pushed the word into the conversation before Chris could reply. He was in business mode again. "Is Dad awake?"

Nora shook her head. "The nurse will be in soon to give him his meds, so maybe you can say hello then."

"We'll wait here. Someone should be with him."

Chris gave his mom's shoulders a comforting squeeze. "If the cafeteria has one of those jumbo cinnamon rolls, smuggle one up to me, okay?"

As soon as the two women were out of earshot, Tim gave Chris a meaningful look. "We don't want to say anything to upset him."

A not-so-subtle hint to toe the Hamilton line, Chris thought wryly.

"No one will give me a copy of the *Observer.*" They were the first words out of Wallace's mouth as Chris and Tim entered the room a few minutes later.

"That's because it increases your blood pressure," Chris said, his voice mild.

"I'm just waiting to see what dirt they dig up next." Wallace shifted restlessly and his intense, dark-eyed gaze flickered over them, pausing to rest on Chris. "Tim said you had a meeting with Felicity Simmons."

Chris nodded. "I'm concerned about the letters she's been getting. It's not your average disgruntled citizen, Dad. Felicity's tires were slashed while she was at work this morning—"

"You don't know that it's related," Tim interrupted. "It could be a coincidence."

"Are you willing to risk Felicity's safety if it isn't?" Chris was frustrated with his brother's tunnel vision.

"The *Observer* is going to have a field day with this," Wallace muttered.

"They won't find out."

"They found out about Jeremy, didn't they?" Wallace's breathing increased and his hand gripped the metal rail on the side of the bed. Chris instinctively reached out and covered it with his own and gave it a reassuring squeeze. As soon as he did, he realized he couldn't remember the last time he'd touched his father. While Nora was affectionate and generous with hugs, Wallace was just the opposite. An occasional, awkward pat on the back was all he could manage to communicate his approval. And there hadn't been many of those for Chris over the years.

"There has to be a way to keep Felicity safe and carry out an investigation without the *Observer* finding out about it," Tim said.

"There is." Wallace continued to stare at Chris. "You can help us."

"I already have. I talked to Captain Driscoll earlier today and told him you would be concerned about the publicity. He promised we could keep a tight lid on this at the department and he officially assigned me to handle Felicity's case."

Wallace shook his head. "It's not enough. If something happens to that reporter, there's no way to keep it quiet. And we can't ignore the fact that the same person who sent the letters to Miss Simmons may have leaked the story about Jeremy to the *Observer.*"

Chris glanced at Tim and saw him nod in agreement. The truth was, he hadn't considered a connection between the two until now. His concern was Felicity's safety. But obviously Tim and his father had.

"I want to hire you," Wallace rasped out.

"Hire me?" Chris wondered if the pain meds were starting to have an adverse effect on him.

Realization dawned in Tim's eyes and a slow smile spread across his face. "He's right. It makes sense. You can keep the investigation in the family *and* keep Felicity safe."

Chris didn't consider himself a slow learner, but they'd lost him somewhere between hiring him and keeping Felicity safe.

Wallace's gaze was riveted on him. "Until you figure out who's writing those letters, I want you to be her bodyguard. Keep a close eye on her."

Chris gaped at him. "I have a job, Dad."

"Until three. Then you're off duty," Tim put in.

Chris wanted to put his brother in a headlock. No, that wouldn't work. He could still talk. "You can't hire someone to be a bodyguard without the other person's permission."

"I'll take care of that." Tim casually crossed his arms.

Chris read his mind. If Felicity didn't agree, she'd be covering the elementary school's summer baseball games. He was about to protest when suddenly he felt pressure on his fingers.

To his amazement, Wallace was squeezing his hand.

"Your chance to help out, son," he whispered. "Maybe it's not so bad to have a cop in the family."

The chance to help. Chris wavered. That's what he'd been hoping for. A chance to show Wallace that even though he wasn't working for Hamilton Media, he was still a valuable part of the family.

It was an answer to a prayer he'd been praying for years.

"I'll do it. But—" he gave Tim a warning look "—let me be the one to talk to Felicity."

Chapter Four

Felicity tried to concentrate on her next assignment but the image of the Cadillac's slashed tires stalked her like the paparazzi chasing celebrities on Oscar night.

What if Chris had been right? What if the person who was clearly a prime candidate for anger-management classes was the same one who'd sent the letters?

For the hundredth time, she silently backtracked through the stories she'd written, searching for something that might have triggered her un-admirer's anger. Other than the mention of the city council meeting, which was open to the public, the letters were so vague it was difficult to pinpoint what might have set him off.

"Go home, Simmons, you're making the rest of us look bad." Lyle poked his head around the half wall, an unlit cigar clamped between his teeth. The cigar had remained unlit for the past six months, ever since his doctor had made him an offer he couldn't refuse— quit smoking or settle into a long relationship with an oxygen machine. Felicity couldn't imagine the temptation that dangling, unlit cigar offered, but Lyle had told her that without it he was like a preschooler without his security blanket. He might not be able to smoke it but he needed it close by.

Felicity looked up at the clock on the wall. Almost six o'clock. Because of Mr. Slasher, she hadn't made it halfway through her to-do list.

"By the way, your ride is waiting for you."

"My ride?" She hadn't called a taxi to take her home yet. The mechanic had told Felicity they had to special order her tires and it would take a day or two to get them in. The downside of owning a piece of history.

Lyle shrugged. "So he says. Ask Herman if you don't believe me. He practically does a background check on anyone who comes to pick up one of his *girls.*"

Any of the single women who worked in the building were automatically tucked under Herman Gordon's protective wing. He might have been old enough to be their grandfather, but he was more intimidating than the principal on homecoming night.

"Even Herman can't kick up a fuss if the guy's a cop, though, can he?" Lyle chuckled and the cigar bobbed up and down. "See you tomorrow, kid."

Chris.

Felicity's heart took a swan dive.

Don't read into it, Felicity chided herself. Maybe he'd found out something about the person who slashed her tires.

She shrugged on her linen jacket and grabbed the

purse she kept stashed under her desk. With her heart still kicking like a stubborn toddler in the candy aisle, she made her way to the lobby.

Herman and Louise had already left for the day and the lobby was empty. Except for Chris. He was leaning casually against the wall and when he straightened, Felicity blinked. He'd packed quite a punch in his uniform, but in faded blue jeans, a white T-shirt and a pair of black canvas high-tops, he was what some women referred to as "eye candy." His dark hair was slightly mussed, too, giving him an appealing boy-next-door quality. The crooked smile he flashed in her direction sent her nerve endings on red alert.

Something was going on. Her reporter's intuition shifted into high gear.

"I called the garage to check on your car and the mechanic told me they were keeping it for a few days. I thought maybe you could use a ride home."

"I didn't realize it was so late. I was planning to call a taxi."

"This will be faster."

In spite of her hunch that there was something fishy going on, Felicity's toes began to throb in her shoes, reminding her that they'd been stuffed into a funnel-shaped pair of flats all day. Another twenty minutes waiting for a taxi might cause irreparable damage and there was a pair of fuzzy slippers with her name on them right inside the door of her apartment.

"Thank you."

Chris grinned and gave a funny bow. "Your carriage awaits, my lady."

She hated the revolving door almost as much as the elevator but at least she could see Main Street through the glass, so it wasn't quite the same as being confined in a windowless moving box.

She pushed through the door, momentarily shoulder to shoulder with Chris, and saw the *carriage* he'd referred to. Tim's lipstick-red Ferrari was crouched in the small parking lot across the street, the one reserved for the Hamilton family.

"Hey, I might never afford one of these but it's nice to have a brother who can." Chris jingled the keys. "He's working late tonight so he told me I could borrow it."

"Is this yours?" Felicity paused and looked at the motorcycle in the parking space next to the sports car. It was an older model but meticulously cared for.

"When I want to claim it."

She saw an extra helmet strapped to the backrest. "We can take this."

If she'd announced to Chris that she'd written the threatening letters herself, she didn't think she would have shocked him more.

"You're serious? You don't exactly look…"

She raised an eyebrow. "Go on."

"I have three sisters. I know when to leave a sentence unfinished." Chris's hands went up between them like a shield.

She didn't budge. She wanted to know what his first impression of her had been.

He gave in. "You just don't look like the type who likes the wind in her hair, that's all."

Ouch. Felicity inwardly winced.

"Are you kidding? I'm from California. I've got two words for you. Highway One." She decided she liked throwing Officer Hamilton offtrack. He shouldn't be judging a book by its cover—or a reporter by her business suit!

"My mother taught me never to argue with a lady." He unhooked the extra helmet and handed it to her. "You might have to…deactivate your hair clip to get the helmet on."

Deactivate her hair clip? Felicity wasn't sure if she should be amused or offended. Guys were clueless about what a woman needed to accessorize! She'd worn her hair long since junior high but when she'd pursued a career traditionally dominated by men, she kept it tamed in a sedate braid or confined in a clip. There were countless times she'd been tempted to get it cut short but so far she'd never quite worked up the courage.

"I'll be fine." She pulled the helmet on *without* deactivating her hair clip, just to show him that it could be done.

Chris swung one leg over the seat and put his foot down for balance, waiting for her to get on. When he started up the bike, Felicity tapped him on the shoulder.

"I need to tell you my address." Her voice was muffled by the face shield.

"You can tell me but I already know it. I have connections." He grinned.

Sure he did. A central database. He probably knew her height and birth date, too. Talk about your cheat sheet....

"Ready?"

She nodded, thinking that the Ferrari looked a bit sulky as they cruised past it.

He had a speech all prepared. He'd rehearsed it while he waited for Felicity to get off work and it was a good one, dealing rationally and objectively with the reasons she should go along with the whole bodyguard decision.

Then she'd picked his motorcycle over Tim's Ferrari.

And he just knew—like he knew that Betty's Bake-shoppe had the best éclairs in Tennessee—that his speech wasn't going to work on Felicity. Just when he thought he was getting a read on who she was and what made her tick, she surprised him.

His relationship with a pretty redheaded reporter was going to get complicated.

In more ways than one.

He'd pulled up Felicity's address on the computer and decided he needed to see for himself what kind of security her apartment had. Her Davis Landing address was in a neighborhood known for its older, well-kept homes. That could either work in their favor or against it. Neighborhoods tended to look out for their own and would notice any suspicious activity, but there was also a homey, "leave your doors unlocked" mentality that could be dangerous.

He turned down her street and pulled his bike up to the curb. Felicity's apartment was an older two-storey brick home, divided into what looked to be upper and lower apartments. He was so busy glowering at the thick bushes that flanked the front door that he didn't realize Felicity had gotten off the motorcycle.

"Thanks for the ride, Officer Hamilton." She pressed the helmet in his hands and headed up the sidewalk.

She was on to him.

He sprang off his bike and followed her up the sidewalk, but before he could formulate a new speech, he was suddenly speechless. The front door was propped open with an enormous purple slipper. Praise music poured out of the opening it created.

So much for security. So much for common sense.

"You live here?" He'd been hoping—no *praying*—she lived on the second floor. Away from a front door flanked by bushes the size of soda machines that practically shrieked, "hide behind me!"

"You tell me." She smiled. A completely insincere smile.

Right. She was still mad that he'd looked up her stats.

"Just doing my job." It was going to become his mantra with Felicity.

She reached down and tugged the slipper out of the door. "Stella? We're home."

Chris checked out the door as he followed her inside. Old. Hollow. One lock that anyone with determination and a twisted paper clip could get into.

"Hey!" An attractive woman with a curly mane of

light brown hair poked her head out of the kitchen. "What's with the *we're…*"

"Stella, have you met Chris Hamilton?"

"Sure." Stella Barton smiled at him and went over to the stereo to nudge down the volume.

He knew Stella from Northside Community and also because of her position as a social worker at Community General. Although she wasn't handling his family's case, he'd seen her in the corridors occasionally and they'd always exchanged a friendly hello.

"I'm just on my way out to ballet class," Stella said. "There's chicken in the slow cooker and garlic mashed potatoes in the oven."

"I love it when it's your turn to cook." Felicity sighed.

Chris watched in amazement as she stepped out of her shoes and wriggled her feet into the purple slippers.

"You're putting on the doorstop."

Stella shot Felicity a guilty look at Chris's comment. "It was the first thing within reach. The air-conditioning isn't working again and I needed some fresh air."

"That's all right. They're versatile." She looked at Chris and shrugged. "A birthday gift from my younger sister. I'll get her back."

"See you around ten," Stella said, grabbing a duffel bag by the door.

"Have fun."

"With twelve six-year-olds? It's a given. Bye, Chris." The door closed with a soft snap. And then bounced open again.

"Bye," Chris said, distracted by the fact that every window in sight was open a good six inches, propped up with an assortment of hardcover books or clay flowerpots. Apparently Stella Barton was the reigning queen of improvisation.

The door closed and Felicity turned to face him, her hands anchored on her hips. "You're checking out my apartment, aren't you?"

"The bulb in your outdoor light fixture is broken. Your windows are beyond outdated and you don't even have a chain lock on the door as an extra precaution." Chris ticked off each thing on one of his fingers.

"It's a safe neighborhood!"

He had the feeling she would have stomped her foot except that it wouldn't have made much of an impact given the fact she was wearing fuzzy purple slippers.

"Felicity, the neighborhood might be safe, but the reality is that *you* might not be." He said the words gently and regretted having to be the one to spark the apprehension that flickered briefly in her eyes.

Her chin tilted in a gesture he was beginning to recognize. "I can't—won't—live in fear."

"We need to work together to solve this."

Her eyes narrowed. "What do you mean, 'work together'?"

Her instincts were as finely honed as his when it came to reading between the lines. He'd take time to admire that quality later. Right now it was a definite liability.

"I talked with Tim and my dad this afternoon. They're hiring me to be your…personal security…after hours."

"A bodyguard!" Felicity's voice changed from its low, melodic alto to a soprano in mere seconds.

"It's the only way. I have to admit we don't have a lot to go on right now. Not even enough to have a squad car cruise past the *Dispatch* or your apartment a few times a day. Captain Driscoll assigned your case to me but Tim doesn't want anything to happen to you."

And neither do I.

"I think you're all overreacting," Felicity said, her voice uneven. "You can't just trail after me, watching me every second. I'll talk to Tim—"

She must have accurately read his expression because her words snapped off. "Tim isn't going to budge on this, is he?"

Chris could almost see the path her thoughts were taking. "It was Dad's idea but Tim backed it one hundred percent."

"Which means if I refuse, Tim will have me writing obits," Felicity muttered. "It doesn't matter what I want. Typical Tim. When I want your opinion—"

"I'll give it to you." Chris finished the sentence with her.

A reluctant smile surfaced and that tantalizing dimple made another appearance. The air whooshed out of Chris's lungs.

"So what does a bodyguard do? Besides annoy the person they're guarding?"

"I've never done this before so I'm winging it," Chris said. "But this 'bodyguard' is going to put an extra lock on your door and order a new air-conditioning unit, which my dad can pay for, by the way. And you better give me your landlord's phone number."

Felicity frowned. "Why?"

"Because I'm going to do some landscaping."

An hour later, Felicity peeked outside and watched Chris hauling the remains of two perfectly good bushes to the curb.

The old adage "money talks" must have a bit of truth in it. The air-conditioning guy had left a few minutes ago, without handing her a bill on his way out. She couldn't imagine what an emergency call in the evening would have cost her and Stella. Cool air pumped into the apartment but didn't do much to bring down Felicity's temperature. Neither did two caramel candies. She was on her third one now.

While Chris had been hacking away at their shrubs, she'd straightened the sofa cushions, fed Sushi, her clown fish, and paced the perimeter of the kitchen. She never paced.

She and Chris needed to have a summit. She valued her independence and wasn't sure she liked the idea of having someone standing in her shadow when she wasn't at work. Not even an attractive police officer that took his job very seriously *and* happened to ratchet up her pulse whenever he was nearby.

Not that Tim was going to give her a choice.

She closed her eyes and ground the remnant of the last caramel candy between her teeth.

Lord, I'm not sure why this is happening. I know You brought me to Davis Landing for a reason. I know You want me to report the truth, but right now there's some crazy person out there who thinks I'm a threat, so they've decided it's payback time. I need Your wisdom. I know You want Your children to be strong…to know that You're in control. Help me not to be afraid.

Felicity drew in a deep breath and breathed out an "amen." The emotions churning inside her began to ebb slightly. Just in time. There was a soft knock on the front door and Chris came in.

"We need to—"

"We need to—"

Their words collided and Felicity shook her head with a slight smile. "We need to stop speaking in stereo."

Chris brushed a hand across his forehead. Even with beads of sweat on his forehead and a smudge of dirt across his cheek, he looked good. If she'd spent the last half hour wrestling shrubs out of the ground in ninety-degree heat, she'd at least *look* like that's what she'd been doing. Sometimes life wasn't fair.

"Mind if I wash up? Then we should talk. I realize having me around is going to be hard on you," Chris said. "We need to come to an agreement about the best way to go about this."

They were on the same page. To Felicity, that was

somehow just as unsettling as being attached at the hip to Officer Hamilton for who knew how long.

"The bathroom is the first door on the left," Felicity said, and then couldn't resist adding, "and there are no other exits in or out, unless you count the hole under the sink where the plaster is coming off."

"Now that you mention it, do you mind if I take a quick look at the rest of the apartment?"

Proving his brain was genetically hardwired to think like a cop.

"I'll give you the grand tour. Just promise you won't take down the trellis on the side of the house. Stella planted the morning glories that are growing on it and she may never forgive you."

He didn't crack a smile. "There's a trellis?"

Felicity sighed. They'd definitely have to come to an agreement.

Chapter Five

❧

It was almost ten when Chris got back to his apartment. When he let himself in, his roommate, Jason Welsh, was hanging upside down from the metal bar riveted to the ceiling of the living room.

He couldn't help but think that their apartment was as appealing as a jail cell when compared to the bright decor in Stella and Felicity's cozy home. It was amazing how inviting real furniture looked in a living room instead of a weight bench and rowing machine. There was a futon here, too, but it did double duty as a place to fold laundry and Chris couldn't even recall the exact pattern of the upholstery.

"Driscoll got you working surveillance tonight?" Jason asked, puffing out a breath between each word.

"No. I picked up a second job," Chris admitted, dropping into a director's chair. It had been a gag gift from some of the other officers on his last birthday—

stamped with the words "You Don't Know Me—Federal Witness Protection Program" on the back.

"Forty-plus hours isn't enough for you?" Jason swung down and landed as agilely as a cat.

"Dad hired me to be Felicity Simmons's bodyguard."

Captain Driscoll had told him they'd keep a tight lid on the investigation but Jason was practically a brother. When Chris attended the tech to earn his degree in Police Science, he'd moved in with Jason, who'd just made his probation at the P.D. Knowing the tension that Chris's decision had created in the Hamilton household, Jason's unexpected offer was another indication to Chris that God was moving ahead of him, clearing the way.

Jason gave a low whistle. "Give me the gory details."

Briefly, Chris filled him in on the letters Felicity had received and why Tim and his dad were so anxious to keep her safe until they found out who was behind them.

"Do you think it's some crackpot trying to scare her or something more serious?"

Chris couldn't help but smile. "She doesn't scare easily."

Jason's eyes narrowed. "I've seen her around. Tall. Red hair, right?"

That didn't begin to describe Felicity, Chris thought, his mind instantly producing an image of her lively, intelligent eyes and thousand-watt smile. "That's her."

"And she's okay with this?"

"I wouldn't exactly say that." *Understatement of the year.* "But she does value her job at the *Dispatch.*"

Jason nodded in understanding. He'd met Tim. "And you want to help out the family."

Chris wasn't surprised at his insight. "At least I feel like I'm doing something. I haven't had any luck tracking down Melissa yet."

"You know you can't fix everything."

"Thank you, Dr. Welsh," Chris muttered, even as he cringed inwardly at the remark. He'd been a cop for seven years and he still struggled with what Captain Driscoll liked to refer to as the "superhero syndrome." He knew he couldn't make the world a perfect place but maybe he was still idealistic enough to want to make it better. Sometimes the bad guys scored a few points but Chris was determined they weren't going to win the game.

"My foster mom always told me I should be a doctor." Jason grinned. "Now that you're moonlighting as a bodyguard, does that mean you're going to bring the reporter with you to shoot hoops?"

Chris slapped a sofa pillow over his head. He couldn't believe he'd forgotten his commitment at Youth Connections. Several evenings a week he and Jason volunteered their time with a sports program for teenage boys in Hickory Mills, an older area of Davis Landing located across the river. They were the ones who'd first seen the need to offer the kids a place to get rid of some excess adrenaline and provide a safe place to hang out, so they'd approached several area churches two years ago and Youth Connections was born.

He hoped Felicity wouldn't be bored, sitting on the bench watching a dozen or so loud, swaggering teenage boys play a testosterone-driven game of basketball.

"Off to the courthouse this morning, Miss Felicity?" Herman Gordon called.

Felicity paused long enough to give him and his wife a quick smile. "Do you have my schedule in your Palm Pilot, Mr. Gordon?" she called back cheerfully.

"My what?" Herman Gordon barked. He lifted his hands and frowned at them. Louise rolled her eyes.

Felicity chuckled, took a deep breath and allowed the revolving door to hold her captive for three seconds before stepping into the sunshine.

She was about to break Rule Number One.

"Don't leave the *Dispatch* without an escort." The other two rules that Chris had spelled out the night before were reasonable. "Deviate from your regular routine whenever possible" and "Document anything suspicious," but Rule Number One would get her laughed out of the newsroom. The last time she'd been forced to pair up with someone, she'd been on a third-grade field trip to Fisherman's Wharf.

Felicity guessed that Chris must have come up with them while he'd painstakingly unwound Stella's morning glories and deposited them into a colorful but tidy heap on the ground. And then removed the trellis.

She'd already bought Stella a box of dark chocolate seashells in apology.

And here she'd thought she and Chris were on the

same page! Color her naive, but when he'd told her they needed to come to an agreement about how they were going to peacefully coexist as bodyguard and bodyguardee, she thought it would be a *mutual* agreement.

She'd decided they needed to have another summit. The sooner the better. She wasn't about to quietly accept Chris's version of house—well, desk—arrest. She conducted interviews with people on a regular basis and several times a week it was her responsibility to go to the courthouse and collect the court news. For the latter, she always tacked on an extra fifteen minutes to stop and chat with Corinne Parish, the city treasurer. In Davis Landing, City Hall and the courthouse were located in the same building, although they operated separately. Corinne, Felicity had quickly discovered, was a veritable treasure trove of information regarding the inner workings of Davis Landing politics.

Which reminded her...

She crossed the street and headed to Betty's. The first time she'd met Corinne, the woman had caught a whiff of Felicity's café mocha and sniffed the air longingly. The next time she'd gone to the courthouse, she'd brought two. It had become a weekly tradition.

"Two café mochas coming up." Betty's daughter, Justine, was working behind the counter as Felicity walked in and she'd already begun to fill one of the medium-sized cups.

This was one of the things that amazed Felicity about life in Davis Landing. After a mere three weeks

Justine had watched her cross the street every Tuesday morning at nine thirty and knew what she was going to order before she ordered it.

Uh-oh.

She'd just broken Rule Number Two. "Deviate from your regular routine."

"Here you go." Justine's sunny smile always accompanied an order. She put in as many hours at the Bakeshoppe as her mother did.

Felicity dug the money out of her purse and thanked her. Resisting the temptation to browse through the shelf of books marked "new arrivals," she smiled at an elderly gentleman who held the door open for her. It wasn't until she was outside that she noticed there were sprinkles on one of the mochas but not the other.

Mmm. She frowned. Maybe she should make a note of that under Rule Number Three. "Document anything suspicious."

She doubted Chris would see anything humorous about her observation. As it was, he thought she wasn't taking the letters or her slashed tires seriously enough. He had a job to do and so did she. She couldn't tell him that if she let herself dwell on the situation, her stomach morphed into a chunk of concrete. Fear would become an invisible wall that blocked out everything else and in her career, she needed to be objective and clearheaded. Chris may have thought he was trying to make her feel safer by turning her and Stella's apartment into a miniature fortress, but it had somehow made her feel more vulnerable.

After Chris had left the night before and Felicity lay in bed, she was still staring at the digital numbers on the clock well past midnight. It was then she realized she was trying to figure out the origin of noises she ordinarily slept through.

In frustration, she'd turned the bedside light on and picked up the leather Bible her parents had given her on her twelfth birthday. She paged through the passages, pausing and slowly reading every one that was highlighted in pink.

"God has a lot to say about being afraid," her mom had told her when she'd given her the Bible. "You may not be able to remember all these verses but all you really have to remember about fear is one word—*don't*."

At twelve years old, it had been a major turning point in her walk with God. A battle in which Felicity had been able to claim—for once—a small victory. She'd worked hard over the years to keep her focus on the truth—that God was with her. That He was bigger than all her fears combined.

She wasn't going to let her creepy un-admirer win. All she had to do was figure out who he was and not only would she be stalker-free, she wouldn't need a bodyguard anymore.

Felicity shook away the unexpected feeling of disappointment that swept through her. The mocha was going to her head. It wasn't like she wanted Chris Hamilton occupying her personal space, was it? No matter how much she admired his dedication to his family. And his job. And the way his caramel-brown eyes had widened in surprise—and approval?—when she'd preferred his motorcycle to Tim's Ferrari. And his engaging smile…

"Bossy. Stubborn. Shrub destroyer. Trellis remover." Under her breath, she began to tally the things about him that drove her crazy instead. The way her heart rate soared when Chris was close by? Now that was something to fear.

"What's his name, darlin'?" Corinne Parish met her in the hallway, right outside the door of her third-floor office.

Corinne was well into her fifties and had been employed by the city of Davis Landing in some capacity since she was twenty. As round as she was tall, she was dressed in her usual eclectic blend of navy polyester and colorful silk. As if the nine-to-five professional had waged war against her inner Southern belle and they'd eventually reached a compromise.

Felicity blinked. Somehow she'd scaled the wide stone steps leading up to the building and had made her way up to Corinne's office on autopilot. Before she could think of a response that wasn't an outright fib, Corinne's nose twitched and she reached for the steaming cup in Felicity's hand.

"Mmm. I could smell this when you walked in the door." Corinne ushered her into the office.

Saved by a café mocha. Felicity hid a relieved smile.

"So what's happening at Hamilton Media these days?" Corinne asked, an avid gleam in her eyes.

"Daily deadlines. Bitter coffee. Stale donuts in the break room. Same old stuff."

"Humph," Corinne said, obviously disappointed. She picked up a tissue and daintily dabbed at the foam on her upper lip.

Felicity's attention was pulled toward voices in the hallway and she glanced up to see Mayor Whitmore walking past the window, deep in conversation with his aide, Ernest Cromwell.

She'd spoken frequently with both men while covering city council meetings and found the mayor to be rather aloof. He was unfailingly polite to her—the epitome of the Southern gentleman—but he was also guarded when she was nearby. Felicity put the blame for that where it belonged—on the *Observer*—which wasn't above turning a simple comment into a controversial headline designed to sell more newspapers.

Together Mayor Whitmore and Ernest Cromwell made an interesting team. When she'd started working as a reporter, Felicity had quickly discovered that some people really did desire their "fifteen minutes of fame." Ernest, with his flamboyant presence, was one of them. He didn't strike her as the type to be content to dwell in someone else's shadow and Felicity wouldn't have been surprised to discover he had political aspirations of his own. Lately the mayor had dropped a few hints that he might be retiring after his current term in office and Ernest would be a logical successor.

"Mr. Cromwell," Corinne snorted softly as the men moved down the hall toward the stairwell. "Who needs a fancy intercom system when that man's voice can penetrate brick?"

The phone rang, saving Felicity from a reply. Corinne reached out to grab it, nearly blinding Felicity as the light reflected off a faux diamond ring the size of a paperweight. *Never got the man,* she'd confided once to Felicity, *but on my fortieth birthday, I bought myself the ring.*

"You have to file those papers by the first of the month," Corinne barked into the phone. "I don't know. Since the mayor decided that's when they needed to be filed, I suppose!" She lowered the phone and whispered, "This is gonna take a while, sweetie. I'll talk to you soon. Thanks for the mocha."

Disappointed that she didn't have a chance to talk with Corinne, Felicity went to the Clerk of Courts to pick up the court news. She had an hour before her morning deadline, plenty of time to get the information she needed.

Yet by the time she finished, she barely had time to wave goodbye to Corinne through the window before she took to the stairs again.

The elevator would be quicker, she reminded herself, even as she sprinted down the three flights of stairs that would take her to the front entrance. Even though she knew it was silly, she just couldn't scrape off the last bit of residue that fear had deposited a long time ago.

When she stepped into the sunshine, the first thing she saw was a police car gliding down Main Street.

Don't let it be Chris.

It was Chris.

And he'd caught her breaking Rule Number One. What was the term for her situation? *Busted.* That's what it was.

"Good morning, Officer." She gave him a cheerful smile and a wave as she strode past the open window of the police car. The expression on his face told her she was going to hear about this later.

At five o'clock, Chris watched the employees empty out of Hamilton Media like a wave of lemmings. He knew the only people left in the building would be his workaholic brother, his dedicated sisters…and Felicity.

Her car was in the parking lot, sporting brand-new whitewall tires, so he knew she was still at work. Even Herman and Louise had exited the building, arm in arm, just a few minutes before.

The extra time gave him a chance to decide his next course of action. Who would have guessed that keeping an eye on a slender, fiery-haired reporter would mean having to strategize a plan with the skill of a five-star general?

In between his usual traffic stops and responding to various calls over the past eight hours, he'd interviewed several people that worked in close proximity to Hamilton Media's parking lot. No one had seen anyone hanging around Felicity's car the morning her tires were slashed.

He'd also driven by her apartment again and made sure that the front and back entrances were locked and the windows were secure.

It was on his way back to the department that he'd seen Felicity skipping lightly down the steps of City Hall.

Alone.

When she'd breezed past him and given him that saucy wave, he'd been tempted to arrest her for jaywalking, just to get her into police custody and out of his hair.

Obviously the suggestions he'd given her the night before hadn't made an impression. She wasn't going to make this easy on him, but he'd been hired to keep an eye on her and that's what he intended to do.

No matter how frustrating, infuriating—

"Take this."

Great. He was distracted by Felicity being a distraction! Somehow, despite his finely honed police officer senses, she was suddenly standing in front of him, holding out her hand.

When he looked down, he saw a crinkly, yellowish-orange cellophane wrapper cupped in her palm.

"You look like you could use one of these."

"A caramel candy?"

"I keep a supply in my pocket. It takes six minutes and thirty-eight seconds to dissolve," Felicity said. "My dad gets the credit for this theory. If you concentrate on the candy, you won't let your temper get the best of you and say things you aren't supposed to."

"Maybe you better give me two."

Felicity smiled a sunny, guilt-free smile. "One at a time. That's the key. Since we're stuck together, what's the plan, Officer Hamilton?"

"As if you plan to follow the plan," Chris muttered as he popped the candy in his mouth and hoped it worked. "Exactly how many of the three suggestions I gave you last night did you break today?"

"Technically? Two. I don't think the sprinkles would hold up as evidence."

Sprinkles? She'd lost him. He held out his hand and she put another candy into it. "Does Tim have a policy that the last reporter hired has to work longer hours?"

"No, it's just that I can process things better when it's quiet," Felicity said. "The newsroom isn't the model of peace and tranquility these days. Plus, I'm working on a feature that Mr. Bradshaw, my managing editor, didn't exactly assign to me."

Why didn't that bit of information surprise him?

It was safer to change the subject. "I thought we'd go out for dinner."

"Don't you usually stop at the hospital after your shift ends?"

"I talked to Mom already and Dad is sleeping. He started to spike a fever this afternoon and Dr. Strickland is a little concerned, since fevers are usually a sign of infection. He advised the rest of us to take an evening off while they have him under observation."

"It's hard to admit your parents are human, isn't it?" Felicity murmured. "While you're growing up, it almost seems as if they'll never get older. Or be anything other than what they are."

Chris thought of his dad, his muscular frame whittled down by the leukemia, and silently admitted she was right. No one in the Hamilton family was ready to picture what their lives would be like without Wallace.

"I see you got your car back." Call him a coward, but he needed to move the conversation to safer ground. He knew Felicity would see right through his flimsy attempt to change the subject. He was beginning to realize that despite her tendency to disregard the rules, she had a sensitive soul.

"One of the mechanics dropped it off earlier today." Felicity nodded.

"Not quite what the average reporter drives these days, is it?"

"Or the average person." Felicity chuckled. She opened the back door and pushed her leather briefcase inside. "It was a gift from my grandpa. He never threw anything away."

"She's a beauty." Chris was looking at Felicity when he said the words and for a moment their eyes caught and held.

"You mentioned dinner." Was it his imagination or did she look a bit flustered?

"I picked up some things from the deli. It's a nice evening so I thought we could snag an empty picnic table in Sugar Tree Park."

"Just because it's a nice evening, Office Hamilton, or are we following Rule Number Two? 'Deviate from the regular routine'?"

Chapter Six

Felicity saw the answer on his face. "That's it, isn't it?"

"Well, it *is* a nice evening," Chris drawled.

"I can't believe you," Felicity said, sending up a quick, silent plea for patience.

"Let's walk." He reached into the saddlebag on his motorcycle and pulled out a white paper sack.

"You're ignoring me." She felt the need to point it out.

"Have another caramel candy."

"I'll need to buy some stock in the company," Felicity muttered under her breath.

She thought he said the word "ditto" under his breath but she couldn't be sure.

Sugar Tree Park was a short walk from Hamilton Media but Felicity rarely took advantage of the quiet refuge it offered the people of Davis Landing. Several *Dispatch* employees used their lunch break to take the walking paths but even though they'd invited Felicity to join them on occasion, she usually chose to eat a sandwich at her desk and work through the lunch hour.

Chris bypassed the amphitheatre where summer concerts were held and headed toward the grove of trees near the playground. On the weekends the park was crowded with families, who took advantage of the well-kept picnic area, and energetic teenagers playing volleyball. Felicity spotted a young couple taking a leisurely walk around Sugar Tree Lake and a boy playing Frisbee with an exuberant golden retriever, but otherwise the park was quiet.

"How does this look?" Chris gestured to a shady spot beneath a tree.

"Wonderful." Felicity sighed her approval. She'd paired a hunter-green twill skirt with a long-sleeved cotton blouse that morning and even though the outfit had been comfortable in an air-conditioned building, now her skin began to prickle in response to the heat.

Chris studied her, a slight frown creasing his forehead. "You're wearing a skirt."

She blinked. "Yes."

"I don't have a blanket or anything to put down on the grass."

"We could use your jacket." Not that she needed anything, but he looked concerned enough that she felt the need to humor him.

She was surprised he was still wearing it. Even though it was made from a lightweight canvas, it still had to be one layer more than was tolerable.

"We can't use my jacket."

Now she frowned. "Why not?"

"I'm wearing my off-duty weapon."

"Oh." For some reason, it disturbed her to know he was carrying a weapon while he was with her. Which was silly, because a gun was as much a part of his uniform as his badge. "Is that really necessary?"

"I hope not."

Felicity sat down on the grass and kicked her shoes off. "What are we dealing with here?"

To his credit, Chris didn't pretend he didn't know what she was talking about. He dropped easily to the grass beside her and began to unpack the contents of the paper bag.

"This is just a hunch right now."

"I'll take a hunch. It beats what my imagination is coming up with," Felicity said simply. "Who knows? Maybe I can use it for an article."

"Stalkers can usually be put in one of three categories. The first kind has an intimate relationship with the victim. If a relationship breaks off, they just can't let go of the other person. Delusional stalkers are generally the kind you hear about on television—the ones who fixate on a celebrity or someone in the public eye. They may have never met the person, but in their mind, they have a relationship with them." His words broke off as she reached into her purse and pulled out a notepad and pen.

"What are you doing?"

"Taking notes." Felicity jotted a few words down and when she looked up, Chris was staring at her in disbelief. "What?"

"Nothing." Chris shook his head and handed her a sandwich wrapped in waxed paper.

"Neither of those two describe what's going on with me," Felicity mused, and then added, "If there is something going on. So, there must be another kind."

"Some stalkers are angry with the person they're harassing," Chris said, his tone measured. "They feel like they've been slighted, cheated, whatever. In their head, things get twisted to the point where *they* think *they're* the victim."

Felicity thought about the letters and had to agree with Chris that this one fit. Like an uncomfortable, itchy wool sweater, but it fit.

"I cover the city council meetings and court hearings the same way the other reporters have in the past," she said, arguing not with Chris but with herself. "I give an unbiased report of who said what, what happened next. When I did the story on the drunk driver, I made sure my sources were accurate. I didn't write a thing that I couldn't back up with facts."

"The truth is, you could be dealing with someone whose idea of 'the facts' is the polar opposite of yours. The kind of guy who brings a bat to the basketball court."

Felicity almost cringed at the word *bat*. Leave it to an athletic-looking guy to create a word picture like that!

"So why not just call me and talk it out? Give me his side of the story. Why threaten me?"

Chris was silent for a moment. "You're being generous when you assume this type of person is rational. This stalker's goal is to get even."

She'd wanted him to be honest. Feeling Chris's gaze on her, she scratched a few more notes while silently asking God to bring her heart rate back to normal.

Don't let fear get the best of me, Lord. You gave me a job to do here in Davis Landing, so I trust that You'll give me the strength to do it. You promised to be with me no matter where I go and commanded me to be courageous, just like You did with Joshua when he was about to face the enemy....

"Felicity?" Chris prompted.

She hoped the smile she gave him looked sincere. "I hope this is roast beef. I'm starving."

He'd just told her that someone might be nursing a serious grudge against her and she wanted to know if he'd bought roast beef.

Chris wasn't sure whether to laugh or buy her a ticket out of the country. Not that she'd go unless she was boxed up in the cargo hold.

Along with his turkey sandwich, he'd just been served a big helping of doubt. Was he overreacting to the letters? From watching Sergeant Evans and Captain Driscoll over the past seven years, he'd learned not to discard his gut instincts. And his gut instinct was telling him that Felicity had become someone's dartboard. It was just a question as to how far whoever started playing the "game" was going to take it.

"How much do I owe you for my meal?" Felicity asked, yanking him back to reality. She'd set the sandwich aside and was already reaching into her purse.

Chris shook his head. "Nothing."

"Bodyguards aren't responsible for their…" Felicity paused. "What *am* I, anyway? Is there a word for it?"

Other than *frustrating?* Independent to a fault? Captivating… Chris put the brakes on the last one. "You're a victim."

In an instant, the humor evaporated from Felicity's eyes. "I'm not a victim."

"Stalking is a crime. You're the victim." Maybe if she understood the seriousness of the situation, she'd cooperate with him.

Felicity shook her head; the stubborn tilt in her chin was back.

"Let supper tonight be my treat," he said. "If it makes you feel better, you can buy the ice cream."

A reluctant smile softened Felicity's lips. "Let me guess. Rocky Road."

"How did you know that?"

"My sisters say it's a gift. I can always guess a person's favorite ice cream. Do you want to give it a try?"

Never let it be said that Chris Hamilton turned down a challenge. "Vanilla."

Her surprised gurgle of laughter was as light and appealing as the water spraying from the fountain in the middle of the lake. "That was beginner's luck. Why didn't you guess chocolate? Aren't all women supposed to be chocoholics?"

"My sisters are," Chris admitted. "And my mom hides chocolate-covered cherries in the cabinet above the refrigerator. She thinks no one knows they're there but the only reason they've been safe all these years is because none of us like them."

"So why did you guess vanilla?"

Chris shrugged. "Conservative. Like your purse."

"My purse?" Felicity rolled her eyes. "You based your decision on my purse?"

"Unpretentious. Conservative."

"Sure, like my '59 Cadillac," Felicity interrupted darkly. "Your theory, Officer Hamilton, is flawed."

"Why did you guess Rocky Road?"

"Heather mentioned that you'd eaten half a quart when you were visiting one day and she didn't get a single scoop."

She was a redheaded practical joker and he'd fallen for it.

"You played me."

Now Felicity grinned. "Keeps you on your toes. What's the plan after ice cream, Officer? Are we going to tear up some more shrubs? Install motion detectors?"

Chris thought that motion lights wouldn't be a bad idea. He'd look into it.

"We could watch a movie." He didn't watch much television but it wouldn't hurt to change his own routine once in a while. Practice Rule Number Two, as Felicity had called it.

She smiled a slow, slightly wicked smile. "I know just the one."

"Indiana Jones?" he asked, suddenly afraid of that smile. "Good guys, bad guys. Snakes. Things blowing up."

"Let's see. You're officially off duty at ten o'clock tonight, so that gives us, mmm, three hours. Just enough time to watch Maria and the captain."

Chris swallowed hard. He had sisters. He recognized those names. And there wasn't a single explosion. *"The Sound of Music?"* he gulped. The term *cruel and unusual punishment* came to mind.

"I haven't watched it for a few months." Felicity rose to her feet and smoothed out her skirt. "Ready?"

Oh, he was ready. He'd brought a level of peace to volatile domestic situations, stepped into the middle of tavern fights and even looked down the wrong end of a shotgun with a convicted felon on the other side. He could handle *The Sound of Music*. And Felicity Simmons.

"I can't believe you made him watch *The Sound of Music!*" Stella collapsed on the sofa, laughing so hard she wrapped one arm around her middle. "But thank you. I couldn't have come up with a more suitable punishment for dismantling my trellis."

"You're welcome." Felicity blew on her knuckles and rubbed them on her shoulder. "Maybe he'll beg Tim to let him off the hook and stick to his day job."

Stella's laughter faded. "I don't know that that's the best idea, either, honey."

Felicity fiddled with the tassels on a decorative pillow. "If those letters would have been sent to Lyle or Glenn, Chris wouldn't be hanging out with them, watching movies all evening."

"True," Stella said. "But it won't hurt you to accept his protection, will it? Just temporarily?"

"He was wearing his gun tonight," Felicity murmured. "He's like a walking reminder that says, 'be afraid, be afraid, be afraid.'"

"No. He's a reminder for you to be cautious."

"I just want to do my job." There was the root of her fear. Not that she was in danger, but that Tim would get tired of dealing with the situation and tell her to pack her bags and go back to California.

"You're one of the bravest people I know, but it's okay to have someone to watch your back. Knowing Chris is there right now should give you *more* freedom to do your job."

Knowing her friend was right didn't make it any easier to accept. "I guess so."

"I guess so." Stella imitated her disgruntled tone with a low laugh.

"I feel so *confined*."

"If I had to pick someone to be confined with, it'd be Chris Hamilton."

"Stella!"

"Hey, any guy that can stay awake through three hours of *The Sound of Music* and hums the words to half the songs gets an automatic ten points on The Keeper scale. He can also microwave popcorn without burning it. Do I have to spell out how incredible that is?"

"He ripped down your trellis."

"In the interest of homeland security."

"I'm going to bed." Felicity headed toward her bedroom.

"You can't *flounce* very well, you know," Stella called after her. "You need more practice."

With Chris in her life, Felicity figured she'd have it down in no time.

Chris watched the lights snap off in Felicity's apartment and some of the tension eased out of his shoulders. After he'd left, he'd parked a block away and spent the last hour watching the goings on in the neighborhood. Other than a guy tinkering on his boat in a garage a few houses away, everything was quiet.

Okay, Lord, tell me what I did to deserve Felicity Simmons. If it weren't for Dad, I'd be resigning from my post, effective immediately. The Sound of Music! *She knows just how to bring a guy down.*

Chris started up his bike and the rush of air on his face as he cruised down the street had a calming effect. Maybe he should just put an electronic ankle bracelet on her and call it a day. Or sneak a GPS into her briefcase.

Just for his own peace of mind, he swung around the block and went back for one more pass. The street was vacant. Even the guy who'd been working on his boat had called it a night.

Wide awake and battling unfounded feelings of unease, Chris took a ride through Davis Landing and slowed down as he passed The Enclave, the condominium where three of his siblings resided. Even though it was after eleven, there was a light still glowing in what Chris knew was Tim's living room on the swanky sixth storey. Amy must have gone to bed already because her apartment two floors below Tim's was already dark. So was Jeremy's.

He wondered what Tim would do if he popped in on him unexpectedly. Probably challenge him to a game of chess or make him watch the numbers rise and fall on the NASDAQ. Amy would fuss over him, offer him something to eat and bluntly ask him why he was at her door so late at night.

He suppressed a smile. None of his family really understood what made him tick. He wasn't sure he could have explained it if he tried. *The blue sheep of the family.* Jeremy, wielding the affectionate but take-no-prisoners humor that older brothers are entitled to, had tagged that label on him when he'd graduated from the academy.

Not that he minded. He knew that Jeremy wasn't implying he was the prodigal son, just that he'd wandered from the fold of Hamilton Media.

Maybe that's how Jeremy was feeling now, times ten. It was one thing to choose a career outside Hamilton Media's brick family fortress, another to find out after thirty-five years that the man who raised you wasn't your biological father.

He was still blown away by the situation. Not only about the truth of Jeremy's birth but also why his parents had kept it from them for so many years. He understood his mom enough to know that she would have agreed to keep it a secret only with Jeremy's best interests at heart. To protect him. Wallace's reasons weren't as clear. Nor was the reason why he'd suddenly decided to bring it out into the open.

Either way, Chris decided it didn't matter. Jeremy was his older brother and always would be. They had more than blood in common—they had a past. And memories. And, when he decided to come back, a future, too.

Chris gunned the engine on his bike a little more aggressively than was necessary and he winced. Maybe if he were Jeremy, he'd have left, too. Over the years, he'd tossed around the idea of taking a job with another department so he wouldn't be expected to show up for the family dinner once a month. It took a five-mile run to warm up after being exposed to his dad's cool treatment at those dinners.

An ambulance's high-pitched wail sliced into his thoughts and Chris realized he was near the hospital now. Maybe it wouldn't hurt to take a quick pass by Community General since he was in the neighborhood. The bike purred quietly as he banked it along the curb and parked, then looked up at the window in his dad's suite. It was dark so Chris hoped that meant his mom had finally gone home to get some sleep.

Ten minutes later, he found himself outside his father's room. The night nurse paused on her rounds and met him by the door.

"He's sleeping. The doctor ordered some blood tests earlier this evening and we're still waiting for the results. Did you want to go in for a minute?"

Chris shook his head. "I don't want to disturb him." After all, he couldn't tell him anything that was going on at Hamilton Media and that's all Wallace would be interested in. "I just wanted…to check on him."

The nurse nodded in understanding. "Mrs. Hamilton went home a few hours ago."

That was good news, anyway. He couldn't resist the impulse to push the door open a crack and look inside. His view was blocked by an enormous vase of daisies.

"Where did the field of flowers come from?" he whispered.

"Those came earlier. From a Felicity Simmons. Do you know her?"

The nurse's innocent question made Chris chuckle.

"Not as much as I want to, but less than I think I do."

She looked at him in confusion.

Thanks to Felicity, he could relate to the feeling.

Chapter Seven

There was a baby monitor sitting on her desk next to the computer.

Very funny, guys.

No wonder Lyle and Glenn had been grinning at each other like fools during their morning meeting with Ed Bradshaw, the *Dispatch*'s managing editor.

She knew better than to take it seriously—she'd been the brunt of practical jokes at the last newspaper she'd worked at, too—but this one was particularly frustrating. Because it was true.

Her hands were still shaking with the force of her emotions. Ed Bradshaw had pulled her off any evening assignments and divvied them up between the two other reporters. He'd tried to be discreet but it hadn't worked. Lyle had shot her an accusing look because the change would put a serious crimp in his tee time and Glenn had simply scowled. But the high-light of the meeting was when Ed asked her to go back into the archives to do some research on river pollution.

The archives!

Busy work. Work guaranteed to keep her inside the building instead of wandering the streets.

She either had Tim to thank or his brother in blue. An *Anne of Green Gables* movie marathon wouldn't be payback enough for this underhanded, sneaky…

Felicity unwrapped a candy, popped it in her mouth and crunched it in half. Once she was able to discuss the situation rationally, she'd go to Tim…who'd have her taking phone subscriptions by lunchtime.

Momentarily defeated, she spent the next hour at her desk and was just about to pull her sandwich out of the drawer when her cell phone rang.

"Where are you, girl?"

Felicity immediately recognized Corinne's voice. And though the question was strange, she answered it honestly. "At my desk."

Corinne's huff of disgust was audible. "I figured that! What I meant to ask is why aren't you *here?*"

"Is something going on?" Felicity quickly scanned her desk calendar and didn't see anything written in the square that should have put her at City Hall over the noon hour.

"Are you the reporter or am I?" Corinne grumbled. "There's something going on upstairs right now. Mayor Whitmore. Mr. Cromwell. Two city councilmen. And some guy in a black suit who looks like a hit man…"

Corinne did have a flair for the dramatic but in this case, Felicity didn't care. The words "there's something going on" were enough to have her snatching her purse and heading toward the door.

"I'm on my way."

"You didn't hear this from me, by the way," Corinne said, just before she hung up.

Felicity scooted past Ed's office and saw him talking on the phone, his back to her. Lyle was at his desk with his headset on, his two fingers plunking laboriously on the keyboard. She heard Glenn's boisterous laugh coming from the break room and quickened her pace.

The place was a human minefield!

She pushed through the door separating the *Dispatch* from the lobby and almost plowed over poor Louise Gordon.

"Land sakes!" The elderly woman began to wobble like an antique vase and Felicity quickly steadied her.

"I'm sorry, Miss Louise," she said, casting an anxious glance over her shoulder. "I'm in a hurry."

"Must be because you're from California," Miss Louise said, her voice threaded with the sympathy she reserved for any unfortunate person who hadn't grown up in Tennessee.

Felicity didn't have the heart to tell her that it had nothing to do with California and everything to do with her Type A personality.

"Are you all right?"

"I'll manage." Miss Louise brushed an invisible speck of dust off her sleeve.

Felicity hesitated and suddenly Miss Louise snapped her fingers sharply, two inches from Felicity's nose.

"Get a move on! A good reporter is always in the right place at the wrong time."

Grinning, Felicity vaulted through the revolving door and headed toward the courthouse.

A black sports car was illegally parked in front of the building and she sprinted around it.

By the time she made it to the oak double doors, Corinne's hit man was just emerging from the building.

"Excuse me." He brushed past Felicity with barely a glance. Corinne's description was accurate. Not that Felicity had ever personally met a hit man, but he sure would have fit Hollywood's interpretation. Mirrored sunglasses. Sharply pleated black slacks and a charcoal-gray silk shirt. No need for a tie—the guy didn't have a neck. He looked vaguely familiar but Felicity couldn't quite place him. She pulled out her camera phone and twisted in place to snap a picture of him. Just as Felicity captured his image, he glanced in her direction. For a split second, their eyes met and held. Casually, she slid the phone into her blazer pocket and sauntered inside.

Okay, Lord, You and I really have to work on this elevator thing because it would save me a lot of time....

She paused outside Corinne's office but the treasurer wasn't there. She'd probably gone to Betty's for lunch with the rest of the employees on their break.

Felicity decided to go to the mayor's office and see

if he was in. Maybe he'd be willing to give her a brief statement as to why he'd called an unscheduled meeting in the middle of the day.

And where he'd hidden two city councilmen and his aide.

Mayor Whitmore's secretary was at her desk, a pale sharp-faced woman who reminded Felicity of a Siamese cat.

"Is Mayor Whitmore in?"

"He can't be disturbed at the moment. Do you have an appointment?"

"I'm Felicity Simmons, a reporter for the—"

"I know who you are, Miss Simmons," the secretary said, a sour look on her face. "I've been instructed to hold all Mayor Whitmore's calls and reschedule his appointments for this afternoon."

"Because of the meeting?" Felicity hadn't gotten anywhere over the years by being timid.

"Meeting?" The lines bracketing the tight seam of the secretary's mouth suddenly deepened.

"With the councilmen? Mr. Cromwell? And Mr.…."

Obviously the secretary hadn't gotten anywhere over the years by stepping into verbal traps, either. "I'm afraid I don't know what meeting you're referring to."

Sure she didn't. Felicity eyed the closed door that separated her from the truth and the secretary rose quickly to her feet, almost taking her out in a wave of gardenia perfume.

Felicity's nose twitched in rebellion and she took a reluctant step back. "Is Mr. Cromwell available?"

"Mr. Cromwell isn't in the building."

And there was probably no one on the city council hanging around, either.

Felicity gave up and fished her business card out of her purse. "Could you please have Mayor Whitmore call this number?"

"Certainly." The secretary's teeth bared in a sugary smile which Felicity knew translated into, *when pigs have wings.*

She stepped into the hallway and heard a soft shuffle. She lifted her face to the stairwell but couldn't see anyone.

"Chris Hamilton, this is all your fault," she fumed silently, taking the stairs to the ground floor two at a time. "You've got me hearing noises and—"

Fear suddenly wrapped a cold hand around her heart and squeezed. Felicity grabbed the banister to steady herself and drew in a deep breath. Every nerve ending in her body had come to life and was standing at attention. Adrenaline poured through her, jacking up her heart rate.

Someone was watching her. She could feel it.

Be strong and courageous!

They were the only words from the verse that her memory could piece together at the moment but she hung on to them with all she had.

She repeated them until she made it to the doors and stepped into the fresh air.

"Hey, Scoop."

Felicity almost jumped out of her skin. Chris was

suddenly beside her, dressed in blue jeans and a woven cotton shirt. Even wearing plain clothes and that crooked smile she was beginning to recognize, he still had a commanding presence.

She was glad to see him. And she wanted to strangle him. "You're off duty today?"

"From *one* of my jobs." One muscular shoulder lifted and fell. "I thought we could have lunch."

Felicity caught her lower lip between her teeth. "Is there going to be a lecture served on the side?"

"Lecture?" Chris repeated, the picture of innocence. "Oh, because *once again* you took off from the *Dispatch* by yourself?"

"That'd be the one," Felicity muttered.

"I'll save it for dessert."

"Deal." Felicity's heart rate eased into its normal rhythm but she wasn't about to give Chris Hamilton's unexpected appearance the credit. "I have an hour."

"Are you all right?"

Felicity tilted her head and saw Chris staring at her intently. She forced herself to meet his gaze. "I'm fine."

"Uh-huh." Doubt edged the words.

"Just surprised to see you here." That was the truth, anyway.

"I'm here, even though, thanks to you, I dreamed I was fleeing Nazi soldiers in occupied Austria half the night."

A smile tugged at Felicity's lips. "Sorry."

She didn't look sorry. She looked…way too attractive, that's how she looked. Every time he saw Felicity, his heart did a weird pole-vault-thing inside his chest.

Today she was wearing another business suit in some sort of gray-and-tan plaid that looked like the kind of thing a person would wear if they were riding a horse in the English countryside, chasing foxes. She didn't wear jewelry of any kind. Not even earrings. Her hair was pulled back in that stuffy clip she seemed to favor but somehow the severe hairstyle only managed to enhance the classic lines of her face. Which reminded him of the cameo brooch his mom liked to wear to church on Sunday mornings.

He found himself wondering how long her hair was when she took the clip out….

"Chris. Is the heat getting to you? You look a little flushed," Felicity said, jolting him off the path his thoughts were careening down.

"I guess so," he murmured, thankful they'd reached Betty's front door. A blast of air-conditioning made a frontal attack as he stepped inside.

Felicity zeroed in on a table in the corner but to Chris's astonishment, she paused so he could pull out her chair. For some reason, he figured her independent streak would have scorned a simple courtesy like that.

"Dad always told me a girl should never take away a man's chance to be a hero," she said, proving he needed to keep a tighter grip on his emotions. Felicity had just read him as easily as she might read one of the books that lined the wall. It was a new experience and he wasn't sure if he should be impressed or uneasy.

"A hero?"

"The good guy. The knight in shining armor."

Felicity took a menu and began to scan it. Caught in the whirlwind of the lunch crowd, it would be a few minutes before Betty or Justine made their way to the table.

"What else does your dad say?" Chris asked curiously. It wasn't the first time she'd mentioned him in that openly affectionate tone and he wondered what kind of man had influenced Felicity.

"He's full of little bits of wisdom." Laughter lit Felicity's eyes and Chris caught his breath. "His motto was 'why reach for the sky when there's a whole galaxy out there?' And of course he's the one who introduced me to the benefits of anger management à la caramel candies."

"Does he know about the letters?"

"No." Felicity's expression shifted as quickly as a cold front settled in before a thunderstorm.

It was a good thing he was used to walking on the edge. "What do you think he'd say?"

Felicity didn't answer because Betty bustled up to their table in her usual efficient manner, apologizing for the delay. She put down two tall glasses of ice water and pulled a pad of paper from her apron pocket, her pleasant smile lingering on Chris for a moment. "What can I get you two today?"

Chris hadn't even looked at the menu yet. He waited to see what Felicity was going to order. Probably something green and leafy with dressing on the side…

"A double cheeseburger with fries. And a dish of vanilla ice cream. With apple pie on the bottom."

Betty beamed her approval and wrote the order down with a flourish. "Chris?"

"That sounds good to me, too." When she was out of earshot, Chris leaned back in his chair. "Well?"

Felicity looked disgruntled that he hadn't forgotten the question. "I don't want Mom and Dad to worry about me. The letters they'd take in stride as part of my job, but the tires...I don't know." Her eyes narrowed. "By the way, was it you or Tim that got me banished to the archives studying river pollution?"

"What?" Chris blinked.

"I've been pulled off my evening assignments, like covering city council meetings, which is going to make it pretty difficult to cover my beat and it's going to put a crimp in finishing my feature—"

"That sounds like Tim," Chris interrupted, palms raised in surrender. "I'd be more subtle."

"Right. Tearing out shrubs is *so* subtle," Felicity growled.

Chris laughed. "Has Stella forgiven me?"

"She forgave you when you suffered through *The Sound of Music* last night," Felicity admitted. "And then she had the nerve to tell me that maybe it was a good thing I had you to watch my back."

That must have stung. Chris gave her a measured look. "Do you agree with her?"

Felicity shifted restlessly. "I can't say I'm thrilled with the situation," she said, her eyes searching his, pleading for him to understand. "This is my dream job. The job I worked six years to get. If God brought me here, I don't believe He'll leave me to fend for myself. I'm not going to let fear rule my life."

Maybe it was time to be as honest with her as she was being with him. "So you see it as a lack of faith that I wear a bulletproof vest to work?"

Her eyes widened. "That's not the same thing."

"Isn't it? If I applied your theory I'd have to argue that God is protecting me, so why should I bother with a vest?"

Felicity's smooth forehead creased. "That's not a lack of faith, it's common sense. There are bad guys out there. You need to do what you can to protect yourself, to even the odds."

Chris's eyebrow lifted slightly while he waited for her to make the connection. He saw the sudden flare of comprehension in her intelligent eyes and he pushed his point home. "The Bible tells us not to be afraid—you're right about that, but fear was hardwired into us by God Himself. Not to rule us, but to protect us. What some guys refer to as *gut instinct* is what I like to think of as God's design. If we sense danger and pay attention to it, we're using fear the way God intended us to. Something, or someone, doesn't feel right and our body reacts to it. We feel that rush of adrenaline. Our heart starts to pound. God put that in us—not to immobilize us or paralyze us but to give us the strength to respond to the situation."

Chapter Eight

Felicity caught her breath. He'd just described the way she'd felt in the stairwell when she'd had the feeling someone was watching her. And she'd been angry about those feelings, never thinking of them as a positive thing. Should she confide in Chris? Maybe he'd think she was turning into a hysterical woman who was becoming afraid of her own shadow. Or worse, he might tell Tim, who'd insist she take a leave of absence. She'd temporarily lost her political beat, what else would she lose if she told him she suspected someone had been watching her?

"We don't know for sure if I'm in danger. With your job, it's a given," Felicity reminded him.

"In my line of work, I do what I can to not only keep myself safe, but other people, too." Chris went on. "I'm not reckless and I never charge into a situation without weighing the cost. My life, the lives of my friends and innocent people—it's not something I take lightly. I've had hours of training and I figure God wants me to use that knowledge the best way I can. Ultimately, though, my life is in His hands. That's the difference. That's the point when fear bows to faith."

No wonder Chris had stepped away from Hamilton Media and gone into law enforcement. He was almost vibrating with the intensity of his beliefs.

Everything inside her resisted the truth in what he was saying even as she fell captive to the passion in his voice. His hands instinctively moved toward hers on the table until their fingertips were almost touching. Felicity stared down at his hands—the kind of hands that looked strong and gentle all at the same time. There was no wedding band on his finger. She'd known he was single, but maybe she had just caught a glimpse of the reason why.

Maybe he'd filled his life with his career the same way she had. With a single-minded devotion that hadn't left a space for another person. So far.

So far?

Felicity was caught up short by that rogue thought. In an effort to squelch the sudden yearning to have someone like Chris to talk to—to share her days with—she blurted out the first words that came into her head. "I never thought of it from that angle before. Could I interview you sometime?"

"That *angle?*"

Judging from the disbelief on his face, she'd obviously chosen the wrong word. It wasn't her fault that something about Chris Hamilton rattled her more than closed-in spaces. "Mom always told me never to let an opportunity pass you by," she said quickly, relieved to see Betty approaching with their cheeseburgers.

"Pearls of wisdom from Mom." He nodded in understanding and Felicity saw the warmth return to his eyes. His mom was Nora Hamilton. If the term "quiet strength" had a picture beside it, Felicity knew it would be Nora's.

"You've heard a few of those over the years."

"A few." He smiled at Betty as she put a bottle of ketchup near his elbow.

"It's funny how those things stick with you, isn't it?" Felicity mused. "The blessings of a close family."

"I guess." The intense emotion that had challenged her to look at her situation from a different perspective drained away, leaving his words curiously flat. "I'm sure you've heard that the Hamiltons haven't exactly been the poster family for support and encouragement lately."

The pain in his eyes cut right through her. Chris was tough and confident, but when it came to his family she'd seen pockets of vulnerability. And it made her respect him even more. She didn't always deal patiently with things she perceived as weakness—in herself or in others—but somehow she knew that the depth of love Chris had for his family was another one of his strengths.

"Close families may stretch during hard times but they never break."

Chris's eyebrow lifted at her feeble attempt to encourage him. "Another Dad-ism?"

"No." Great. Now she was going to look like an idiot. "I saw it on a bumper sticker once."

Chris's laughter came from some reservoir deep inside him and Felicity knew that only the Lord could keep those wells brimming when life threatened to suck them dry. She swiped a French fry through a pool of ketchup and waggled it at him. "Don't laugh at me."

"I'm laughing *with* you." He winked at her and she felt it down to her toes.

She leaned forward slightly, aware that Betty was clearing the table across from theirs. "Chris, I've heard the way Amy and Heather talk about you. Heather calls you her rock. And your mom brags about you to anyone who will listen."

"Eavesdropper."

"Reporter."

Betty paused beside their table and Chris reached out his hand, assuming she was going to give them the bill. Instead, she gave his hand a little pat.

"It's important for families to appreciate each other," she said. "Their strengths and weaknesses."

Chris nodded in agreement but the glance he shot at Felicity was confused. "That's true."

Betty released his hand. "You take care, Chris. You're a good man. And give my best to your family."

There was silence as she moved away and Felicity reached over and took one of his fries. "See. You have a fan club."

"Interested in running for president?"

"What will that get me besides a cheap button and the envy of all my friends?"

"Meet me in the parking lot after work and I'll show you."

Chris spent two hours with his parents at the hospital. While Nora took a walk around the grounds to stretch her legs, Wallace had grilled him about Felicity but without his usual level of agitation. Chris was almost afraid to believe that maybe it meant his dad had a small measure of trust in his abilities. At least it gave them a common bond, something they hadn't had since he was a kid and he'd coaxed his dad into the backyard to play catch.

When Heather showed up, she'd freed him to head back to the *Dispatch*. And hopefully to Felicity.

She had a gift for sneaking out on him, and even though she'd been cranky about being taken off her evening assignments, Chris was glad Tim had done it. It was obvious she was more than capable of causing enough trouble during the day!

He could only pray that he'd gotten through to her during their conversation at the Bakeshoppe. It had been divine intervention that he'd suddenly thought to use his bulletproof vest to make his point. But would she admit to him if she were afraid? Would she even tell him if something spooked her? Or if she received another threat? He couldn't be sure. She trusted God to protect her but she didn't trust him. Not yet.

When he'd met up with her on the courthouse steps,

he could have sworn by the way she reacted to his un-expected appearance that something had made her jumpy.

Probably you, Hamilton.

Their relationship was forged out of necessity and they were still finding their footing. Coming from completely different perspectives but trying to fit together. No wonder they were laughing one minute and nose to nose, glaring at each other, the next.

When he got to the parking lot, he noticed that Felicity's Caddie wasn't anywhere in sight. With a sinking feeling, he stalked around the opposite side of the building to look for it. The only thing he saw was an ancient bicycle, the kind he'd seen in movies that sported a wicker basket on the handlebars. Which this one did.

"Rule Number Two. Deviate from your regular routine," Felicity sang out as she emerged from the back door of the building and zeroed in on the bicycle. "I left my car at home this morning."

Call him a cynical cop, but Chris wondered if it was safer for her to be recognized at the wheel of a blue Caddie the size of an armored vehicle or riding a rickety bicycle, at the mercy of someone in a car. Someone in a car with a nasty grudge.

"It's from my grandpa—"

"Let me guess. The one who never threw anything away."

"That's right. Are we going back to my apartment to watch another movie?"

Chris winced. "Not tonight."

Felicity looked disappointed. "Stella and I had one all picked out."

"I'll bet you did." Chris was relieved it was a Youth Connections night. "I have a commitment that I can't get out of and I hope you don't mind coming with me."

Felicity's eyes narrowed. "Is this going to be a guy thing?"

"You could say that."

"You're getting even for *The Sound of Music*, aren't you?"

"That never crossed my mind." But hey, if it worked.

"Since I don't think I'll fit in this basket, we'll take my car."

"You have a car?"

Was she teasing him? It wasn't a Ferrari but it got him from point A to point B. Felicity locked up her bicycle and then slid into the passenger's seat. He'd noticed she wasn't one of those women who marinated themselves in perfume, but occasionally he caught the scent of the soap she used. Like right now. The soft fragrance reminded him of a piece of his childhood—the way his sheets had smelled after drying on the clothesline in the summer sun.

He headed toward the bridge over the Cumberland that separated Davis Landing from Hickory Mills and noticed with amusement that Felicity was leaning forward, eagerly watching the scenery as if she was trying to guess where they were going. He suppressed a smile. Apparently her inquisitive nature had been put to good use!

"So why did you decide to be a reporter?"

"When I was a freshman, I hurt my knee and got sidelined from sports. My parents suggested—in a loving way—that I find something else to do besides mope around and drive everyone crazy. I tried chorus. The teacher politely told me to try band. The band teacher steered me toward the school newspaper."

"Where you discovered your inner busybody."

She flashed him a look. "Ouch."

"Sorry." Chris forced a smile. "Reporters have been permanently crossed off my Christmas card list this year. I'm not used to my family's private life being open for inspection. Or should I say *dissection?*"

"That wasn't professional journalism," Felicity said in disgust. "In fact, it bordered on libel. That's why I like to concentrate on local government. There's a lot that goes on behind the scenes and if reporters aren't there to give objective coverage, integrity might take a back seat. We keep things honest."

"You realize that most people wouldn't buy your argument that reporters keep things honest. They'd say the media like to slant things for their own agenda."

"That's where my faith comes in," Felicity said simply, not rising to the bait. "Ultimately, I answer to God for the things I write. He keeps me on target."

They were a lot alike, Chris thought in amazement. He ran into the same kinds of potholes in his profession. Guys that went into law enforcement because they were the neighborhood bullies all grown up and still loved to push their weight around. Or they started out with what Felicity had called integrity and then the focus shifted from what they could do for the community to "what's in it for me?" Dirty cops. He'd run into a few of those over the years.

It was a constant challenge as a believer in his career not to grow cynical while he traced footprints into the dark places where some people chose to walk. Jason understood. He hadn't expected that Felicity might.

"What's this place? Don't tell me—it's witness protection à la Tim Hamilton." Felicity pressed her face against the glass, peering through the rain at the row of identical brick buildings that huddled on a bend near the river.

"Not quite." Chris eased the car into the narrow space tucked beside one of the buildings. Now that they were here, his heart kicked up a notch. How would Miss Button-Up react to the group of energetic, and sometimes unruly, boys he coached? Maybe he should have asked Jason to run things tonight.

"Hey, bro. It's about time." A small, wiry figure as thin as a pogo stick bounced in the doorway and waved to them.

"Jason and I run a sports program for kids a couple times a week. It's only two hours. I know you'll probably be bored out of your mind, but grab a chair and maybe I can hunt up a magazine…" He knew he was rambling but Felicity was already getting out of the car and he felt the sudden need to warn her. The shrill, grating laughter of boys who teetered on the edge of puberty and the sharp thud of basketballs bouncing off the rim rushed out of every crack in the building.

The look Felicity turned on him would have melted steel. "A *magazine?*"

Chris didn't have a chance to respond because they were surrounded by a cluster of sweaty adolescent boys, all talking at once. It reminded Felicity of watching a nominated actor on the red carpet before the Academy Awards—except that every question pelted at them began with one word: Chris.

Felicity took advantage of the commotion to look around. The cavernous room had been transformed into a gym. The hardwood floor was scuffed and worn, the water-stained walls plastered with posters of famous athletes. Fans chugged in the corners, circulating the humid air.

"Is this your *girlfriend?*"

The question rose above the others and Felicity suddenly felt the weight of a dozen pairs of curious eyes.

Chris grinned and deftly caught the basketball that one of the boys lobbed at him. "Nope. She's my cheerleader."

His cheerleader? Felicity's eyes narrowed. First he was going to bench her with an issue of *Nashville Living.* Now he planned to arm her with a pair of invisible pompoms.

Not in this lifetime, Officer Hamilton.

Jason came out of a back room and blew a whistle. "Shirts against skins. Teams are the same as last week."

A cheer spiraled to the top of the plaster ceiling and T-shirts were tossed into the air like confetti, landing in damp little heaps at the boys' feet. They sprinted toward Jason and by lifting one hand above his head, he separated them with the same flair she imagined Moses must have used to part the Red Sea.

"Come on, Chris!" A chorus of impatient shouts ricocheted around the room and Chris shrugged a silent apology as he loped away to join them.

"Your stuff might be safer in the back room," Jason called out to her, motioning toward an open door at the back of the gym.

Felicity followed the direction he'd pointed in and wandered into a makeshift locker room. Wooden benches were scattered around the room, layered with discarded lumps of clothing and discarded shoes.

She dumped her bag on one of the benches and pulled out the black cotton shorts and T-shirt she'd stuffed inside, the ones she'd worn when she'd ridden her bicycle to work that morning. Wiggling her feet into heavy white socks and a pair of tennis shoes, she unclipped her hair and shook it out. She didn't have a brush along, so she finger-combed it and pulled it back into a casual ponytail.

When she stepped out onto the gym floor, Chris was dribbling the ball toward the basket, a swarm of boys at his heels. His lean body twisted gracefully as he went in for a lay up. And then his eyes met Felicity's.

He missed the basket. And landed with a resounding smack on the floor.

Felicity hurried over to him and knelt down. The boys crowded in around her.

"Are you okay?"

"That's gonna leave a mark," another one breathed in awe.

"You lost your focus, Chris," the boy crouched beside Felicity complained, obviously lacking the sympathy his friends had.

"I don't think he lost his focus," Jason said. "I think it just went to something other than the net."

Felicity glanced up and saw his amused gaze resting on her before he grabbed Chris's hand and yanked him to his feet.

Chris rubbed his side and smiled wanly. "I'm fine. Just got a little distracted."

"It's our ball," one of the boys shouted, right next to Felicity's ear. She recognized him as the boy who was bouncing in the doorway. On the back of his wrinkled T-shirt, the name Pepper had been stamped in block letters.

"I play center," Felicity said.

"Chris said you were a cheerleader," one of the boys was brave enough to grumble.

"I'll tell you what. If I make five free throws in a row, you'll let me play."

Everyone forgot Chris as the boys raced to watch her take her place at the piece of soiled white tape that stretched across the floor at the free-throw line.

Chris limped up to her just before she took the first shot. "By the way, when you mentioned you got sidelined from sports in high school, exactly what sport was it?"

Instead of answering him, Felicity let the ball go. There wasn't a sound as everyone watched it sail through the air and swish effortlessly into the net.

He shook his head. "I thought so."

Chapter Nine

"Do you need some ice? Or maybe a clue?" Jason slapped Chris's back as the boys counted out Felicity's next four shots, each number increasing in volume as she sunk every single one of them.

Chris couldn't answer. He was distracted by the gentle swing of Felicity's ponytail, which lay against the middle of her back like a satin rope. Those sedate business suits she favored had effectively concealed the trim build of someone who was extremely physically fit. But it was more than that. They'd concealed the feminine curves of a woman, too. The black shorts and the yellow T-shirt were modest enough to wear to the mall but there was no denying that he was seeing Felicity in a whole new way.

He swallowed hard, still in shock at the unexpected transformation.

Jason gave him a good-natured shove. "Focus, Hamilton. It's not like you've never played coed ball before."

"Um. Right." Jason was never going to let him forget about this. One glimpse of Felicity's porcelain skin and his vocabulary spiraled down to Neanderthal level.

Jason rolled his eyes and knocked the basketball out of Chris's hands. "Okay guys, Felicity's in. Let's play ball."

An hour later, the game ended in a tie. His ribs still aching from their close encounter with the gym floor, Chris met Felicity at the cooler, where the boys were helping themselves to bottled water.

"You're full of surprises, aren't you, Scoop?" he murmured.

"So are you." Felicity's glance swept meaningfully over the boys, who panted in a loose circle around them. "I've seen Youth Connections mentioned in the church bulletin but I didn't realize you and Jason were involved in it."

"It was our baby," Chris admitted, not quite able to keep the note of pride out of his voice. "A few years ago, there was an increase in delinquency. Kids hanging around after school, getting into trouble. Graffiti on the bridge. Underage smoking. Things that can get out of hand if no one takes any action. Jason and I played ball with a men's league but we decided if we were going to put the time and energy into the game, we'd rather go for a bigger return."

"I can see why."

"Northside Community and some of the other

churches have been really supportive of our efforts. Once a month we put out a call for volunteers."

Felicity heard the subtle question in his voice. If she loved the game, why hadn't *she* ever volunteered?

Because I put my time and energy into my career, that's why.

With Chris's curious eyes focused on her, Felicity was reluctant to voice the thought out loud. She'd rationalized that her new job at the *Dispatch* called for a season of sacrifice while she proved herself. Convinced herself that when the special feature she'd been devoting every spare minute to was completed—the one she hoped would turn her byline into a signature political commentary—she'd be able to get to the rest of the things on The List. Like accept more dinner invitations. Organize her photos. And volunteer for a church ministry or two. Like Youth Connections.

"This is great. What you're doing here." It was safer to comment on what Chris was doing instead of what she *wasn't.* Suddenly Felicity began to question whether all the reasons she'd come up with were simply excuses in a workaholic's manual somewhere.

"Yeah, well, it's easy to get attached to the little buggers."

In spite of the description, Felicity heard the warmth that pulsed through his words.

She'd seen the hero worship on the boys' faces as they basked in Chris and Jason's attention. Even though there'd been times during the game that the two men had had to give out warnings when some of the adjectives got a little colorful, the boys had accepted the discipline without complaint.

Jason's whistle pierced the air. "Let's call it a night, guys."

To Felicity's amazement, instead of scattering, the boys gathered around Jason.

"Prayer time. I'll be right back." Chris jogged over to the cluster of boys and waited until their excited chatter subsided.

"Lord God, You gave us a place to get together and have fun but You know that outside this door, life isn't so easy. Walk with us. Give us wisdom when we have to make tough decisions. Remind us every day that You love us. Give us the courage to love You back."

Felicity's eyes were burning when Chris finished the simple prayer with a heartfelt "amen." She'd never heard a prayer quite like it but it stirred something inside her. Strong and honest, just like the man who'd prayed.

"Pepper, make sure all the towels are picked up in the locker room. Mark, it's your turn to empty the trash." Jason strode toward the doorway and a ragtag group of boys fell in behind him.

"A little old-fashioned responsibility mixed with the fun?" Felicity murmured as Chris returned.

"It's their program so it gives them a sense of ownership if they have to pitch in and help." He paused and smiled wryly. "In theory, at least."

"It's a good one." Felicity heard the good-natured

grumbling as the boys disappeared into the locker room but she noticed Pepper's swagger as he lead the way. "Is basketball the only sport you offer?"

"Basketball is our big draw right now," Chris said. "We want to expand our program, though, and eventually have the place open every night. Jason wants to coordinate a youth Bible study midweek and we'd like to offer special events on the weekends."

"And the No Girls Allowed sign on the door?"

Chris frowned slightly and Felicity sighed. "Okay, so it's invisible. But you have to admit you've got nothing but Y chromosomes lumped together in here."

"Temporary, we hope. We need women to volunteer so we can offer volleyball or basketball to the neighborhood girls. Interested?"

Felicity should have seen that one coming a mile away. "I haven't played for years." Not since college, when she'd earned some extra money by coaching a girls' camp during the summer.

"It doesn't look like you've lost your touch."

She picked up a basketball and spun it on her index finger, considering his comment. "You think?"

Chris pulled a sweatshirt over his head and when his face emerged, he was smiling. "Let's just say you're the one with the fan club tonight."

Felicity's looked more closely at the gym. "Are you going to have enough room here to do everything you're planning?"

"We've rented for the past few years but recently the committee that oversees the ministry put in a bid to buy this building and the two empty ones right next door. It was definitely divine intervention that I found out this whole corner was going up for sale. We can get it for a pretty fair price because it's in such poor condition."

"Whoever owns it should pay you to take it off their hands," Felicity teased.

Chris shook his head. "You never know. A few months ago I talked to a woman who was interested in buying one of the buildings on this block to house a domestic-abuse shelter similar to one in Nashville. They were forty-eight hours from closing the deal and the next thing they knew, the building was taken off the market."

Felicity silently filed away the information he'd just shared with her. Somehow, that bit of news had slipped past the *Dispatch*. "What do you think happened?"

"This side of Hickory Mills can be a bit rough," Chris said cautiously. "Some people might be in denial that this area needs a domestic-abuse shelter. Then you have the other end of the spectrum—people who think that opening one is the equivalent of saying 'there goes the neighborhood.' I have no idea why the owner decided not to sell. The building is still sitting there empty."

"I'd think the city would want the buildings fixed up instead of watching them crumble into the river. It would only add to the value…and they'd be put to good use."

Even as she said the words—as logical as they

sounded—she knew that local governments were hot-
beds of opinions and conflicting interests. She'd interviewed Mayor Whitmore enough to know that he
walked a fine line in Davis Landing. He genuinely
cared about its citizens and his willingness to use tax
dollars to make a better life for them was the proof.
Judging by the heated debates at the council meetings,
not everyone agreed with his priorities.

"Taxes on a building like this don't exactly fill the
city coffers." Chris laughed, but it sounded forced.
"They'd probably make more money if the buildings
were razed and sold as lots."

"You've got Pastor Abernathy's support and it
sounds like a few other churches have come on board.
You aren't in this alone." Felicity paused. "You may
have to rally the troops but you can't forget Who's in
charge."

How did she do it? Felicity had a knack for cutting
right to the heart of a matter. Or for reading his mind.

Either one left him feeling off center. He hadn't
meant to share his concerns with her. He hadn't even
told Jason how unsettled he'd felt after talking with the
woman who was interested in buying property for a
domestic-abuse shelter in the neighborhood. There was
no basis for his unease—the owner of the building at
the end of the block wasn't Roland Sykes, the man
who owned the three buildings they wanted to purchase
for Youth Connections. He reminded himself that God's
hand had been moving all along—the number of boys

coming to play basketball had doubled in the past six months. He'd talked to several area coaches who seemed intrigued by their vision and were thinking about offering their time to run some day camps in the fall. He was in a constant state of awe at the work God was doing on River Street.

"Hey, Hamilton, the boys went out the back but you better make the rounds just to be sure. Lock up when you leave, okay?" Jason emerged from the locker room and tossed the keys in Chris's direction. "I have a date with ESPN at nine o'clock."

"No problem." Chris caught the keys with one finger as they sailed within an inch of Felicity's ear. She didn't even flinch.

"Is it a double date?" she murmured.

Chris grinned in reply. "Maybe. First I've got to make sure we've got an all clear. One night, one of the kids decided not to go home and ended up crashing here for a few days."

"How did you find out?"

"The mountain of empty soda cans was suspicious. Rats prefer candy and, just between you and me, they have a little trouble with pop tops."

Felicity giggled. He'd never heard her giggle before and the sound carved a path right through him.

"I'll bet they do." Her eyes were lit with humor, her cheeks still flushed with color. Until now, every time he'd seen her she was dressed in her business best with her hair scraped away from her face. She was still beautiful, but beautiful like a statue in a museum—you could admire it but not touch it. Somehow, wearing old gym clothes and with her hair caught back in that loose ponytail, she was not only breathtaking—she was approachable. He resisted the urge to brush a damp strand of silky hair off her cheek. Instead, he shoved his hands in his pockets and retreated, keeping a few steps between them.

Felicity followed him into the empty locker room and reached for the bag on the floor. When he'd noticed it slung over her shoulders, he hadn't realized she was hiding workout clothes in it. The lady was full of surprises.

He checked the bathroom and straightened up some of the wire baskets that lined the wall.

"Did I mention we want to update the plumbing and add some showers?"

"No." Felicity's nose wrinkled. "But I think that's a great idea."

She sat on the bench and Chris noticed she was fumbling with something. "Did your watch break?"

"No. I took my bracelet off before the game." There was a small frown of concentration between her eyebrows. "The clasp can be temperamental."

"Let me see." Chris stepped closer to see what she was doing. "Wow."

She slanted a look at him. "What?"

"It's a…bracelet."

"Ah, didn't I just say that's what it was?"

She had, but Chris had expected something simple. Something serious. Made up of tiny gold links. This one was…*girlie.* There were fascinating flashes of pink and aqua and yellow in the midst of the sterling silver figurines.

"It's a charm bracelet," Felicity explained, her tone just prickly enough that Chris knew she'd noticed his disbelief. "Mom started it when I was five years old and every year after that, she bought a new one for my birthday. She tried to find a charm that signified something that happened in my life that particular year."

"So it's like the purple slippers your sister bought you for your birthday." Chris understood. There was a garish orange-and-blue tie he still had that Melissa had bought him one year—and made sure he wore occasionally. "One of those gifts you wear out of obligation."

"Are you kidding? I love it." She looked offended.

He couldn't believe he hadn't noticed it before. It even jingled when she turned her wrist. Then he remembered that Felicity usually wore a jacket or long-sleeved blouse to work, hiding it from view. From what he could see, it didn't exactly fit her image. He studied the bracelet. Not a single miniature computer. Or tiny desk. What he saw was a colorful jumble of Felicity's life. And it was fascinating.

Peering closer, he saw a tiny silver basketball hanging next to a fish. A surfboard. One of those old-fashioned quill pens. And a lion.

"A lion? Did you run away and join the circus?"

Felicity fingered the tiny animal. "No." When she

answered his teasing question, her voice was soft. "I should go home now and get some sleep. You know, recover from the three minute free-for-all you guys called overtime."

She took a step away and Chris felt her sudden withdrawal. A strange sense of loss chased through him in its wake.

"Let me try to do that." His fingers weren't exactly designed for persnickety jewelry clasps but Felicity stood patiently while he worked at it. "There you go."

"Thanks." Felicity's voice was brisk again and they walked to Chris's car in silence.

She reminded him of a puzzle that Amy had bought him one year for Christmas. The picture looked simple enough—one of those popular landscapes that people liked—but when he'd opened it up, every piece was the same shape. It had taken him the entire winter to figure it out.

The streetlight ignited the fiery glints of red and gold in her hair and the faintest whisper of a breeze drifted off the river. Felicity lifted her face and closed her eyes. Welcoming it.

Had she paid attention to anything he'd told her about being aware of her surroundings? It was dark. They were in a neighborhood near the docks. He'd deliberately parked close to the entrance but the shadows had crept in, shrouding everything in gray.

And she was standing in the open with her eyes closed, enjoying the hint of a breeze on her face.

"Felicity." His voice was curt and her eyes snapped open. "Are you paying attention to your surroundings?"

"Is this a quiz?" she asked mildly.

His teeth ground together. "Pepper and one of his friends are spying on us from behind the dumpster over there. A tomcat is stalking a rat that's almost as big as he is by the doorway over there. The car parked across from mine is empty…except for the person passed out in the backseat."

Felicity blinked at him. Then she smiled. "You forgot to mention the woman watching us through binoculars from the second-storey window up there."

He glanced up just in time to see the curtains drift shut. "Okay, maybe you were paying attention."

"I'm a reporter, Chris. It's my job to notice a lot of things. We aren't that much different if you think about it. Truth and justice. Spaghetti and meatballs."

Spaghetti and meatballs? How was he supposed to respond to that?

Just as he reached out to put the key in the ignition, Felicity's hand covered his.

"I'm going to talk to Tim," she said, her voice even. "If I don't get any more threatening letters in the next week, I'm going to ask him to fire you. I'll be careful. I passed your quiz, didn't I?"

Chris tamped down his rising frustration level. How could he explain to her that a stalker didn't plan weekly appointments with the person he was victimizing? The fact that she hadn't received a letter in the past few days didn't mean that someone wasn't watching her. Taking notes on her daily routine. Learning about her so he would know where she was vulnerable.

"What about your tires?"

"We haven't linked that to the stalker," Felicity said. "I saw a dozen kids tonight that looked perfectly capable of indulging in that kind of entertainment."

He couldn't exactly argue with that. Half the boys she'd played basketball with already had a juvenile file at the P.D.

He tried another tactic. Sometimes he had to switch out of cop mode and become someone else. Confidante. *Friend.* He gave her a casual smile and put on his best southern drawl. "Are you saying you don't like hanging out with me, Simmons?"

Chapter Ten

Chris's question was still ricocheting around Felicity's head the next morning when she got to work, making it extremely difficult to concentrate. Which was exactly why she didn't want to spend every evening with him.

She'd seen right through that police academy training maneuver he'd tried out on her as he drove her home. If he couldn't bully her into accepting his protection, he'd charm her into it. And no doubt about it, Chris Hamilton could pour on the charm. She'd worked for Hamilton Media for several months—shoulder to shoulder with drop-dead gorgeous brothers Jeremy and Tim Hamilton—and listened with amusement to every sigh from the single women employed there whenever they were in view. Yes, they were attractive, confident men from a wealthy family. But she could sign an affidavit saying that she'd never sighed when they smiled at her.

But Chris…

She sighed.

"Simmons!" Ed Bradshaw roared the word in her ear and Felicity jerked her headset off.

"What?"

"Are those things making you deaf?" Ed's eyes were practically bulging out of their sockets. "What were you doing up at City Hall yesterday?"

Uh-oh. "I got a call about a possible meeting."

"Who called?" He aimed the end of his pen at the center of her forehead.

"I can't say."

"You can't say," Ed repeated. "I'm the editor, for crying out loud! *You can say.*"

Someone must have switched his coffee from decaf to regular when he wasn't looking. "An employee." That's the best she could do. She wasn't going to get Corinne in trouble for giving her a heads up, even if she'd gotten the facts wrong.

"Where's the story?"

"The mayor's secretary denied there was a meeting."

"Really." Ed's left eye began to twitch. "That must be why she called and said that one of my reporters was harassing her yesterday."

A polite inquiry was harassing? Since when? "She's exaggerating. I asked her about the meeting and she said she didn't know what I was talking about."

"Let's just put the whole meeting-that-wasn't aside for a minute and concentrate on the fact that you were supposed to be up to your freckled little nose in back issues, looking up those stories on river pollution that I asked you for." Ed's voice had a tendency to start out at a yell and then lower until the last word rumbled out like the lowest note on a tuba. Felicity had never known anyone who yelled *backwards* before and it was always fascinating to listen to.

"I was about to get right on that, Mr. Bradshaw." Freckles? No way. He was so upset he was probably seeing spots in front of his eyes.

He glared down at her. "By Monday."

"Monday." Felicity nodded agreeably. On the inside, she was imagining her career being sucked down the drain. And Tim and Chris Hamilton waving goodbye while they watched it disappear.

When he stomped back to his office, Felicity dialed Corinne's number.

"City Treasurer." It was an unfamiliar voice that answered Corinne's extension.

"Corinne Parish, please."

"Ms. Parish is unavailable. Can I help you?"

"Do you expect her back soon?"

"Ms. Parish is on vacation."

"Vacation?" That was just weird. One of the things that Corinne loved to talk about was her annual two-week cruise to the Bahamas every February. She'd mentioned that even though the cruise used up every second of her vacation time, it was worth it. "This is Felicity Simmons from the *Dispatch*. Can you tell me how long she'll be gone?"

"I don't know." Irritation had leached into the

woman's perky voice and Felicity could practically see her tapping her fingers against the crimson, rose-shaped blotter on Corinne's desk.

"All right. Thank you, Ms.…."

The phone went dead. Felicity stared at the receiver for a few seconds, trying to process what had just happened. It had to be a coincidence that Corinne messed up her facts about a meeting and then decided the next day to take an extended vacation. Without mentioning it to her.

And why had the mayor's secretary called her boss to complain she'd harassed her? There *had* been that tiny fraction of a moment when she'd contemplated vaulting over the desk and storming the mayor's office to find out the truth…but she didn't want her beat permanently assigned to Lyle or Glenn. If that happened, she might be…mmm, sifting through the archives looking for articles on river pollution?

"We're heading over to Betty's in a few minutes for a sandwich. Want to come along?" One of the women who worked in advertising paused at Felicity's desk.

"I can't today. Mr. Bradshaw has me working on a special feature."

"You work too hard, Felicity. Are you sure he doesn't have you handcuffed to your desk?"

That would be something Chris would do, Felicity thought darkly. She pasted on a smile and lifted her wrists. Underneath her sleeve, her bracelet jingled softly. "See? I'm here of my own free will."

"If you change your mind, we'll be there."

Felicity's lion peeked out of the bottom of her cuff and she tucked it back in, remembering the shock on Chris's face when he'd seen it. Maybe a charm bracelet was kind of kitschy but she'd always loved it. Every one of the colorful charms was linked to a memory, a piece of her childhood. Her mom had stopped buying the charms when she'd turned eighteen, telling her that she could fill the last few spaces on the bracelet with symbols of the things that meant the most to her.

So far, she hadn't added any more. She hadn't had time.

Chris had asked her about the lion but she wasn't ready to share that part of herself with anyone.

Maybe if you'd told him, he'd understand why you aren't going to let fear affect your life anymore.

Like a zealous defense attorney, the thought sprang up and confronted her.

That's between You and me, isn't it, Lord? I can understand why Chris wants me to be cautious and I will, but I'm going to trust You. Lion's den faith. That's what Dad said I should have. Just like Daniel.

"Hey, Simmons." Lyle sauntered past her desk. "I know Hamilton's a slave driver but take some time to smell the roses. Or at least have a cup of coffee."

"Thanks for the tip." Felicity lifted the baby monitor in a jaunty salute and Lyle laughed.

One by one, the employees disappeared to take their lunch breaks. Felicity nibbled at her roast-beef sandwich as she began her search through the back issues. Occasionally the fax machine would hum to life as a story came over the AP wire service, but the newsroom was usually quiet after the paper went to print. In the afternoon, the reporters worked on the next day's articles or conducted interviews for upcoming stories.

It would have been helpful if Ed had told her how far back he wanted her search on pollution to begin…as far as wild-goose chases went, this one would definitely win a prize for being the most creative. She decided to start at the beginning of the New Year and go from there. Maybe she could use Ed's underhanded method of keeping her under house arrest to do some additional research on the feature about the debate over community development she'd been working on for the past month.

Using her mouse to scan quickly through a January issue, Felicity paused as one of the headlines caught her attention.

RiverMill Developers Draws Criticism from City Council.

RiverMill Developers. That was a name she was familiar with. Wes Greene, the CEO, was on her list of people to interview for her feature. She'd heard his name at city council meetings because he was an aggressive proponent of "off with the old, on with the new." Which meant that his wrecking ball didn't hesitate to destroy a piece of history if it meant his financial portfolio got thicker. At least that's what she'd overheard one of the councilmen complaining about at one of the meetings.

She skimmed the article, which had been written by the reporter she'd replaced in May.

RiverMill Developers, owned by millionaire investor Wes Greene, has recently come under criticism from several city councilmen because of statements Greene made regarding the local historical society's recent decision to apply for a grant to restore the bell tower in the historic Mansfield building. In a letter to the city council, Greene apologized for calling the society an "antiquated group of senior citizens with no vision for the future."

No wonder he had to publicly apologize, Felicity thought. The historical society was a force to be reckoned with. Felicity knew that in the past few years they'd saved an old church, that had once been part of the Underground Railroad, from being demolished.

Felicity's finger hovered above the mouse and then clicked the print key on the toolbar. As the printer began to hum and click, she typed in the words *RiverMill Developers.*

And suddenly Corinne's hit man appeared on the screen.

She couldn't believe it. He was in the foreground of the photo, almost shielding a man standing directly behind him. Felicity quickly scanned the caption, which identified him as Wes Greene's attorney. So why had RiverMill's attorney been at City Hall? Felicity didn't believe in coincidences.

After a quick scan through the yellow pages, she

dialed a number. Wes Greene had just moved to the *top* of her list.

"RiverMill Developers."

"May I speak with Mr. Greene, please?"

"One moment."

Felicity was put on hold and three times a new voice picked up her request. Finally, she must have made it to the president's personal secretary.

"I'm sorry. Mr. Greene isn't available. If you leave your name and number, someone will call you back."

Someone. Not necessarily Mr. Greene, though. Felicity tapped her pen quietly on her desk as she calculated the best way to get the information she was looking for…in a way that would still allow her to sleep at night.

"Maybe you can help me." She injected enough perky enthusiasm into her voice so hopefully she'd seem as threatening as a teddy bear. "Mr. Greene was scheduled for a meeting with Mayor Whitmore yesterday…"

Felicity banked on the fact that people weren't comfortable with silence. She'd discovered that if she started a sentence, most people were happy to finish it. Especially busy people like personal secretaries.

"No, I'm sorry. Mr. Greene was in Nashville yesterday visiting a job site. There is no record of a meeting with Mayor Whitmore."

"Oh." She laughed, letting embarrassment seep into her voice. "My mistake. Thank you."

"Your name and number," the secretary repeated, her voice suddenly wary.

"That's all right. I was just calling to inquire about the meeting but if there wasn't a meeting…" One vacuous giggle coming up. "I must have been misinformed."

"You must have been." Now the woman's voice was cold enough to quick-freeze Sugar Tree Lake.

"I won't take up any more of your time. Thank you." Felicity hung the phone up and rubbed the back of her neck.

The phone on her desk rang and Felicity picked it up. "*Davis Landing Dispatch*. Felicity Simmons."

There was silence on the other end. Then a decisive click, as if the caller got all the information he or she needed when they heard Felicity's voice.

Felicity closed her eyes. She didn't like unanswered questions. Ed expected her to have something about river pollution on his desk by Monday and Chris was going to be waiting for her in the parking lot when she got off work. Which left the window of opportunity on complete lockdown.

She searched her pocket for a caramel candy and came up empty. Then she remembered that she'd put her last one in the console of Chris's car the night before…right after she told him she was going to have him fired next week.

"Any developments on the Hamilton case?"

Chris looked up as Lou Driscoll paused at the table where he was writing up a complaint. As usual, his captain's tie was slightly askew and one of the tails of his shirt had come untucked. Even though he had the slightly rumpled look of a modern-day Columbo, Chris knew there was nothing casual about the way the captain viewed his responsibilities. He knew everything that was going on with his officers, professionally and personally.

"Nothing yet." They were alone so Chris knew they could speak freely. "It's been pretty quiet so far. Maybe the person got tired of the game, took his ball and went home."

"You don't sound convinced." Driscoll ignored the empty chair next to Chris and rolled his large frame onto the edge of the table instead.

"Felicity—Miss Simmons—thinks that a few days without any contact means she's right—the guy is just an angry but harmless citizen blowing off some steam and wanting to be sure people notice it."

"That's a dangerous assumption."

"Exactly what I told her." Chris still fluctuated between anger and amusement every time he remembered her bold assertion that she was going to ask Tim to fire him.

"Doesn't sound like she's paying much attention to your instincts, Hamilton."

The laughter in his voice made Chris suspicious. If the captain knew anything about his relationship with Felicity—one based on mutual frustration—there was only one person who could have leaked the information. Jason.

"Yes, sir."

"Maybe if there is someone watching her, they're having second thoughts about continuing the threats now that you're in the picture."

Chris had thought the same thing, which was enough of a reason to stay with Felicity after she got off work and into the evening. He'd read through the articles she'd written again and compared them to the letters. So far, he still couldn't come up with anything that might have set someone off. Not that an irrational person needed much of a reason.

His radio crackled to life, yanking him into the present.

"I need an officer to do a welfare check on an elderly woman who's not responding to phone calls from her family this morning," the dispatcher said. "Address is 314 Magnolia. The daughter is worried because her mom refused to turn on the air conditioner they bought for her."

Judging by the weather predictions he'd heard on the way to work that morning, Chris suspected this call would be the first of many over the next few days. August temperatures could be brutal and there were a lot of people who didn't have central air or simply refused to use it in order to keep costs down.

"Ten-four. I'm on my way." With a quick nod to the captain, Chris headed toward his squad car. Jason met him at the front door and they fell into step together. Jason was also a licensed EMT so if there was someone who needed immediate medical attention, Chris was always glad to have him along.

"What have you been telling Driscoll?" Chris growled as he slid into the driver's seat.

"I need more details, buddy."

Seeing the grin on Jason's face, Chris knew he didn't. Still, he had to humor him. "About Felicity."

"I think I might have mentioned that you haven't been exactly…how should I put this? On your best game lately. A bit distracted, if you ask me."

"I didn't ask you."

"See, your sense of humor is gone, too."

"She's driving me crazy." Chris finally admitted.

"Crazy like you're starting to fall for her?"

Chris's foot stomped on the accelerator and the squad car lurched forward. *"No!"*

"Whoa." Jason put his hands on the dash and pretended to brace himself. "If you're going to drive like a professional racer, at least warn me first. And it was a simple question."

How could he put this into words his lunatic roommate would understand? "Crazy like she doesn't pay any attention to the fact she might be in danger. Crazy like she keeps sneaking out of the *Dispatch* during the day while I'm on duty. And so what if she notices that there's a woman with binoculars? She still closed her eyes. *That's* how she's driving me crazy."

"Okay, you officially lost me after the binoculars."

"She doesn't listen to me."

"And of course that would drive a control freak like you crazy. I get it now."

"I'm *not* a control freak," Chris muttered. "I just don't want anything to happen to her."

"Uh-huh."

Out of the corner of his eye, Chris saw Jason's smug expression. "I don't want anything to happen to *anyone*, Jase. That's why I'm a cop."

"Sorry I jumped to conclusions," Jason said, not looking a bit sorry. "Your dad and Tim asked you to protect her. It's what you do. That's all it is. I got it."

"Good," Chris muttered, turning the squad car into the driveway of the house they'd been called to.

Watching Felicity was part of his *job*. There were a dozen other things he could be doing on the evenings he was off duty instead of listening for the internal mental bell to signal his next verbal sparring match with a stubborn reporter. Like spending more time at the hospital. Calling volunteers for Youth Connections. Fixing the leaky sink in the bathroom.

The only reason he was anxious to see her again was to make sure she stayed out of trouble. *Not* because he actually missed their verbal sparring matches when he wasn't with her. Or because he couldn't stop thinking about her.

Chapter Eleven

Five minutes before she went home for the day, Felicity's feet began a nervous tap dance under her desk. She told herself that it had nothing to do with the fact that Chris was probably waiting for her in the parking lot.

So far in his attempt to "deviate from the regular routine," he'd taken her on a picnic to Sugar Tree Park, then to play basketball at Youth Connections. As she gathered her things, she wondered what he was planning for this evening. In her world—prior to the one which now included a bodyguard—evenings when she wasn't covering a meeting were usually spent curled up on the sofa watching a video…or playing a cutthroat game of Scrabble with Stella.

Get a grip, Felicity! You aren't dating the man. He's doing this as a favor to his father and brother. It's not like he'd spend time with you if he had a choice….

The lights flickered suddenly and Felicity frowned,

automatically reaching for the mouse so she could shut down her computer.

"Simmons, could you run this upstairs to Mr. Hamilton?" Ed stopped just long enough to dump a folder of papers on her desk. "If I'm late for our ballroom dancing lesson, my wife is going to strangle me with my cummerbund."

Ed Bradshaw in a cummerbund. Felicity tried not to grin at the visual. "Sure."

"Did you find those articles I asked you for?"

"Three so far." *And one interesting link between Wes Greene's lawyer and Mayor Whitmore?* She wasn't ready to mention that to Ed yet. If her intuition was right, maybe she could incorporate some of this new information into the feature she was writing about the ongoing power struggle between two camps—the people who thought community development meant helping the people who made up the community and the ones who thought it was measured by the number of new tax dollars they could bring in.

"Great, great." Ed mumbled the words as he strode away.

Felicity glanced at her watch and hoped Chris wasn't waiting for her in the parking lot. If he were, by the time she found him he'd be melted to the concrete.

She walked into the lobby to tell Chris she'd be a few more minutes but there was no sign of him. The thought that he was roasting in the oppressive heat while she took the stairs to Tim's office made her hesitate in front of the elevator.

"Okay, Lord, we can do this," Felicity breathed. "Fifteen seconds. Twenty at the most."

She pressed the button.

There was a low hum as the elevator rumbled down to where she waited. Clutching the folder tightly in her arms, she waited until the door opened and then she launched herself inside. Without giving herself time to think, she located the oversize button marked with the number three and punched it.

The elevator door closed.

And everything went black.

By the time Chris got back to the department, he'd put in two hours of overtime holding Mrs. Sherman's fragile, blue-veined hand while she was treated for heatstroke at the hospital.

Just as her daughter had feared, the elderly woman hadn't wanted to "waste" the air-conditioning so the temperature in her tiny house had risen to a dangerous level. When Chris and Jason had broken in, they'd found her in the living room, collapsed on the floor.

They'd immediately called for an ambulance and when Chris had held her hand, Mrs. Sherman didn't seem inclined to let it go when she came to. He'd left a message for Felicity at the *Dispatch,* telling her he'd be late and that he'd meet her at her apartment as soon as he could.

That had been over an hour ago.

"Chris, your brother is on the phone," the dispatcher said as he walked past, more than ready to write up his report and leave for the day.

Jeremy? Hope arched inside of him. It had been more than a week since Chris had heard from him and even though he'd left several voice messages, his oldest brother hadn't returned his calls. "I'll take it in the back room."

"It's Tim and it's not a personal call. He's asking for assistance."

"Let me talk to him." Chris's mouth went dry as he took the phone. "This is Chris."

"We've got zero power in the building," Tim said, his voice curt. "I assume it's the entire block…do you have any idea what's going on?"

"Just a second." Chris glanced at the dispatcher. "Has anyone else on that side of town called yet?"

She shook her head. "Not yet."

Within five minutes, Chris found out that none of the other buildings on the block had lost power. Dread formed a cold knot in his chest as he thought about Felicity. As late as it was, he tried to convince himself that she would have gotten his message and gone home by now.

"Are you the only one still inside the building?"

"Felicity's car is still in the parking lot," Tim said, splintering Chris's assumption that she was safely at home.

"I'm on my way."

Chris used both his lights and siren to clear a path through the traffic. He parked the squad car and Tim met him at the front entrance.

"Did you find Felicity?"

"She's stuck in the elevator," Tim said quietly. "I can't get her to talk to me."

Felicity huddled in the corner of the elevator, her arms wrapped protectively around her middle and her eyes squeezed shut, closing out the darkness.

Her breathing came out in shallow puffs and she felt a trickle of perspiration weave a crooked path down the side of her cheek. In the past fifteen minutes, she'd alternated between praying for strength and biting her lip to keep from screaming for someone to open the door.

As the seconds ticked by, she tried to bully herself into believing that it was silly to be afraid when there was no threat. She wasn't the only person in the building. Someone was probably already working on the problem and if she didn't panic, the electricity would come back to life. The air-conditioning unit in the building must have gone into overdrive and short-circuited every wire in Hamilton Media.

She repeated every rational reason why she shouldn't be afraid and forced herself to open her eyes. And could almost see the walls begin to close in around her....

Lord, please help me hold it together here. I can't remember my verses for courage. I need Your strength...

"Felicity? It's Chris."

His voice was muffled on the other side of the door but just hearing it eased some of the tension in her shoulders. She edged closer to the sound, although her arms and legs felt heavy, like she was moving under water.

"You can't play hide-and-seek with a cop. We always win."

Felicity winced. Hide-and-seek. That's what had started her aversion to confined spaces to begin with.

"I hate that game."

Chris didn't realize he'd been holding his breath until he heard Felicity's faint response.

Thank You, Lord.

"When are you going to get me out of here?"

The words tugged at him when he detected something he'd never heard in her voice. Fear.

"We're working on it." He leaned closer so she could hear him better. Only five minutes had gone by and already he felt like a sponge. Navy-blue polyester wasn't exactly a breathable material in one-hundred-degree heat. Technically he was off duty so he loosened his tie. If he was this uncomfortable, he could only imagine how Felicity was feeling.

He needed to distract her until the electricity was restored. "Why do you hate hide-and-seek? Did you lose once?"

Silence. Chris swiped his arm across his glistening forehead and waited.

Come on, Scoop. What's going on?

"Actually, I found the perfect hiding spot."

Chris reached up and touched the door, splaying his

fingers out against the surface, wishing he could see her face. The unmistakable tremor in her voice was still there.

"Sorry." He kept his voice upbeat. "I don't see the problem."

"I was visiting relatives and Mom asked me to baby-sit my cousins for a few hours. We started playing hide-and-seek with some of the neighborhood kids. The people who lived next door had a crawl space under the house and we figured no one would find us in there."

"It sounds like a good place to hide." A little warning siren began to go off in his head.

"It would have been. Except for the earthquake."

Earthquake? He was almost afraid to pursue the conversation he'd started. The one he'd hoped would take her mind *off* the fact that she was trapped in an elevator. He decided to take a risk because he sensed she needed to talk about it. "What happened?"

"The usual. Chaos. The walls buckled. Things fell. My cousins were six and I was twelve, so I couldn't exactly fall apart."

Judging from her tone, that's what she'd wanted to do. Chris tried to imagine Felicity in such a terrifying situation at such a young age.

"How long were you in there until someone found you?" He had to ask.

"Only a few hours."

Chris's breath hitched. Only a few hours. It must have seemed like forever. "Someone found you, though. And your cousins weren't alone. I'll bet you were glad you were with them."

There was a curious silence and just when he was about to knock on the door to coax a response, he heard her voice, weighted with frustration. "Chris, I hate small spaces now. But you know what's worse? I *hate* that I hate them. For a few months after the earthquake, I couldn't sleep. I didn't want to go anywhere. Mom started reading what she called the Lion Verses to me. Scripture that reminded me Who was in control and encouraged me to not be afraid."

Suddenly he remembered the lion on her charm bracelet. And the way she'd withdrawn when he'd teased her about it. No wonder she'd wrestled with accepting his protection. She'd battled with fear and because of her faith she'd triumphed—but with his unwelcome presence in her life now, it must seem as if she was fighting for the same territory all over again.

Chris wondered if she even realized what she was revealing.

One of the other officers knelt beside him. "We checked the entire building and there's no sign of anything suspicious. The breaker box wasn't tampered with, either."

"Thanks, Joe." Chris lowered his voice. "How much longer?"

"The electrician said a few more minutes."

After he walked away, Chris tapped on the door. "How are you doing in there?"

"I can think of other places I'd rather be. *Larger*

places." Even under stress, Felicity's resilience peeked through.

Chris suppressed a smile and suddenly the lights came back on. The elevator made a clunking sound and the door opened agreeably.

And Felicity stumbled into his arms.

Felicity felt Chris's arms go around her and for a split second, she allowed herself to lean against him. She hadn't meant to tell him about that piece of her past but, strangely enough, sharing it with him had somehow loosened the grip it had on her in the elevator.

Except now he probably saw her as one of those clingy, needy women who hid in the shadows instead of walking in faith, confident in God's protection.

"I'm sorry." She stepped away and he immediately released her, which probably had something to do with the fact that Tim and two other police officers were striding toward them.

"Are you all right, Felicity?" When she saw Tim's forehead was creased with concern, Felicity realized that she was probably a mess. Because of the heat, she'd shed her jacket in the elevator and even though she was wearing a modest camisole underneath it, she still felt vulnerable. Damp strands of hair brushed against her neck, a sure sign that her hair clip had failed to keep them confined.

She took a deep, steady breath. "I'm fine."

"I brought you some water. Maybe you should sit down for a few minutes." Tim handed her a bottle of what Stella liked to call "designer water." She didn't care about the label as long as it was wet and cold.

"No thanks." Felicity shook her head firmly. "I've been sitting long enough. I think I just need some fresh air."

She didn't miss the look that Tim and Chris exchanged. Two Hamilton knights in shining armor were ganging up on her.

She wanted to run to the revolving door and out into the open air, but made herself walk at her normal pace. Chris didn't hover at her elbow but allowed a few feet of space between them as he walked with her.

How was it that he seemed to know exactly what she needed?

"I've got to go back to the department and wrap up a few things," Chris said. "I left in kind of a hurry."

For the first time, Felicity realized he was still in uniform. "You're supposed to be off duty."

"I ended up working some overtime today because of a sweet but stubborn lady who didn't want her electric bill to go up. Just when I was about to leave, Tim called about the power outage."

For the first time Felicity noticed that his entire body was tense—his eyes alert as he scanned the parking lot. "You thought the blackout had something to do with my un-admirer, didn't you?" She saw the answer on his face and it squeezed the air out of her lungs. "You're being paranoid."

"And you're being naive."

They glared at each other.

"I'd like you to come to the department with me and

then I'll take you home." There was a definite edge in Chris's voice that raised her hackles.

It didn't sound like he was giving her a choice.

"I feel like being alone tonight." She knew she was being unreasonable—but so was he!

"Fine."

"Fine."

She got in the squad car and the trip to the police department seemed to take forever. Chris ignored her and Felicity seethed beside him. How could she have thought for a second that Chris Hamilton was a sensitive man? If someone were going to try to get to her, they wouldn't cut the electricity in an entire building to do it! They'd...*what would they do?* She wasn't sure but she did know that Chris was taking it way too seriously.

Paranoid! Chris gritted his teeth. He couldn't believe she'd accused him of that. Cautious. Streetwise. Aware. He'd accept any of those descriptions. But paranoid? No one had ever accused him of that before.

"I'll be back in a few minutes," he muttered. "My bike's parked over there."

Felicity didn't answer and out of the corner of his eye he saw that her chin had that familiar, stubborn tilt. She also looked totally wrung out, which made his heart soften just a little. She'd gone through more than an uncomfortable half hour in a dark elevator. She'd had to relive a traumatic experience from her past and it showed on her face.

But apparently it hadn't stripped away her frustrating tendency to want to handle everything by herself.

He strode into the department and almost plowed into the Captain, who was leaving for the day. "I heard you check in. Is your reporter safe and sound?"

His reporter. That was the punch line of the day, Chris thought darkly. "She's fine," he managed, keeping his voice respectful.

"Dispatch said you ran lights and sirens through town."

Was his boss implying that he'd overreacted to the situation, too? Great. His reputation for keeping a cool head on the job was being sunk. Sunk because all he could think of on the way to the *Dispatch* was that someone could get to Felicity if he wasn't there to watch her back.

"Hamilton Media was the only building with no electricity. It seemed suspicious."

"Uh-huh." Driscoll slapped him on the back and Chris didn't miss the amused expression on his supervisor's face as he turned and shuffled toward the door. "Have a nice weekend, Hamilton."

Chapter Twelve

After Chris dropped her off at her apartment, Felicity found a note from Stella written on the chalkboard in the kitchen, telling her she'd gone to visit her mom for the evening.

Feeling less than human from her ordeal, Felicity showered and changed into drawstring cotton pants and a matching T-shirt in a vibrant lava-lamp orange. Ordinarily, the cheerful fabric lifted her mood, but not tonight. She flopped down on the sofa and closed her eyes.

In spite of the words she and Chris had exchanged, she'd wanted to thank him for staying with her while she was trapped in the elevator. Even before she could open her mouth to say the words, he'd offered a clipped goodbye and left.

Alone with her restless thoughts, she had to face the truth. She'd called him paranoid for assuming the worst but for a few terrifying moments in that dark elevator, she'd wondered the same thing. Wondered if the person who'd written the letters was finally acting on his threats. As a cop, Chris dealt with the underbelly of society every day and it had probably become second nature to tune into anything suspicious. He'd simply been using the training that kept him safe in order to keep *her* safe. And she'd called him paranoid.

How could she have explained to Chris what she'd really been feeling when she didn't understand it herself? His soothing voice on the other side of the elevator door had strengthened her. And when the door finally opened, she realized that the comforting circle of his embrace could easily become her refuge if she let it.

Felicity groaned and slapped a pillow over her face, slightly muffling the sound of the telephone as it rang on the coffee table in front of her.

"Hello?"

"This is Mrs. Mitowski across the street," a woman's nasal voice informed her. "I don't want to seem nosy but I thought I should tell you there's a strange man lurking around your apartment. Do you want me to call the police?"

Felicity's heart gave an answering thump and she rushed to the window. The sight of the familiar figure in the yard only slightly eased her heart rate back into its normal pattern.

"Thank you, Mrs. Mitowski, but I know this particular lurker."

Felicity bit back a smile and wondered if there was

some kind of daily *stubbornness* quota that Davis Landing police officers had to fulfill. After winning a brief battle against the lock on the window that Chris had insisted she and Stella start using, she pushed it open and leaned out. "I distinctly remember you saying that you were going to leave me alone."

"I am." He dropped down on the small square of grass that served as the front yard and promptly rolled onto his back, his muscular frame stretching out to his full height. He covered his face with an open book and crossed his arms under his head, a sure sign he planned to stay for a while.

"It's too hot out there."

His response was to give her a thumbs-up sign. She rolled her eyes and marched outside, stopping six inches from his shoulder. The title of the book draped across his face caught her eye. *Dead by Midnight.* Now there was some nice, light reading. "Don't you have something more exciting to do than camp out on my doorstep?"

"Not a thing."

"If you want to turn yourself into the main course of a barbecue, I'm not going to stop you."

He lifted one corner of the book and peered up at her.

"How many caramel candies have you eaten in the past hour?"

She crossed her arms. "Four."

"Six."

She wasn't good at holding a grudge and apparently, neither was he. Their eyes locked and held for a moment and then they both started to laugh.

Felicity flopped down beside him and plucked at the blades of grass. The minute of silence that stretched between them wasn't an uncomfortable one and that surprised her.

"I'm sorry, Chris. I'd like to say I wasn't being myself a while ago but that wouldn't be true. I *was* being myself. That's the trouble. I can be a little outspoken at times."

Which she knew might have something to do with her weekend plans involving a video and pizza. Wasn't that what Lance, her ex-boyfriend, had warned her would happen?

"You'd just gone through a tough situation," Chris said. "All that emotion needed an outlet."

Felicity sighed. "An outlet, maybe, a target, no."

Chris heard an undercurrent of tension in her voice and wondered about its source. The blackout had put him on edge, too, but the image he couldn't erase from his memory was the vulnerable look in Felicity's eyes after she'd stepped away from him. Paranoid or not, he wasn't going to leave her alone for the rest of the evening. He'd gone back to his apartment to change his clothes and then called the hospital to check in with his family. Amy had sent Nora home and was staying with Wallace the rest of the evening.

Offering a quiet prayer of thanks that things seemed to be quiet on the home front for the moment, he'd gone back to Felicity's for the rest of the evening, uncertain of his welcome.

Until she'd laughed with him.

"I'm protected from bullets, remember? Even the verbal ones." Even though Chris wasn't wearing his vest, he thumped his chest just to see if she'd smile again. It didn't work. He sat up and tossed the book onto the grass, studying her. "You're being too hard on yourself."

"And you're being too nice. I'm outspoken and independent…"

Chris touched her hand without thinking and felt her jolt of surprise. "You say those things like they're negative. God knew what He was doing. You need those qualities to be a good reporter."

She nodded but her gaze shifted away from him. "A good reporter, yes, but they're not exactly the warm, fuzzy qualities that someone wants in a…"

She caught herself at the last moment and almost choked, suddenly horrified that he'd fill in the blank. She'd been about to say "wife." Felicity couldn't believe how easily Chris scaled her defenses. Like they didn't even exist.

"I think they're good qualities for anyone to have," Chris said with a shrug, unaware that she was about to race back to her apartment and bolt the door.

Not according to Lance, Felicity thought. And Lance was a man, so he must have had the inside track as to what men were looking for in a mate.

She'd been a senior in college when she'd met him at a bonfire her church organized for young singles. He was everything she hadn't known she was looking for and they'd clicked immediately. They'd spent a lot of time together and Lance had seemed supportive while

Felicity sent out her résumé to newspapers in the area. Then one night, close to graduation, he'd asked her to meet him for dinner at their favorite restaurant. As Felicity spent an extra hour preparing for the evening, in a tiny corner of her heart she wondered if he planned to propose.

Instead, he'd broken up with her. And kindly told her to consider that God might be calling her to a life of singlehood. Her strong personality was a little too intimidating. Her independent streak wasn't attractive. Men wanted to be needed and it just didn't seem like she needed anyone.

When she'd taken a long, hard look at the woman she was—and was becoming—she knew he was right. And because her parents had raised her to accept the woman God had created her to be, she knew she needed to accept that her personality didn't mesh with a man's idea of a perfect mate. In some ways, Lance's honest assessment had freed her to focus even more on her career, although there were some Friday nights when she silently admitted she was lonely and she wished that Lance had been wrong.

"Okay, give me his name and date of birth." Chris's sudden growl pulled her out of her reverie. She blinked and Lance's face—with his soft, apologetic smile—was swept away. Now she was nose to nose with a riled police officer.

"Who?"

"The guy you were just thinking about. The clown who obviously fed you a bunch of lies." Chris had seen the same look on Melissa's face after she'd had her heart broken by some loser who couldn't see what a treasure she was.

"Just because someone tells you something you don't want to hear doesn't mean it's a lie," Felicity said, her even tone telling Chris she'd accepted the guy's twisted philosophy without question. Her next words confirmed it. "He was right. Men want women who are soft, feminine. The kind who nurture people, not interview them. It's just a fact of life."

Somewhere in California there was a guy without a clue who needed to get *his* facts straight, Chris thought, anger simmering close to the surface.

"Um, Chris, you're going to permanently indent a starfish into my wrist." Felicity winced and he quickly loosened his grip on her hand, leaning over to inspect the damage he'd inflicted.

"Sorry," he muttered, rubbing his thumb gently over the mark he'd accidentally made on her wrist as he pressed the charm into her skin. Her very *soft* skin.

Not feminine? How could she believe that? Just because she wore business suits to work didn't mean she was denying her femininity. His sister, Amy, dressed in a similar style when she came to work. There was a gentle side to Felicity and the proof was in the dainty charm bracelet that jingled on her wrist under those conservative blouses. And the fuzzy purple slippers she wore because her sister had given them to her. And the way her eyes had softened when she'd asked about his family the first day they'd met.

Not nurturing? He'd seen firsthand how Felicity had interacted with the boys at Youth Connections. By the end of the evening, they were her champions. She'd even reeled one of the younger ones into an impulsive hug and ruffled his spiky blue hair. He'd blushed and pulled away, but for the rest of the evening Chris hadn't seen his feet touch the floor.

It wasn't Felicity's fault that some guy hadn't appreciated the different facets of her personality—maybe he'd simply been too lazy to look below the surface. To Chris's way of thinking, whoever had wounded Felicity had been the weak one. He didn't think there was anything threatening about a strong woman. He pictured his mom and sisters. Even gentle, sensitive Heather had blossomed in the past month, their dad's health crisis refining her when it might have crushed someone else.

He struggled to find the right words in an effort to do damage control. Whoever the guy was, Felicity must have cared about him or his words wouldn't have made such an impact. It was up to him to make her see the truth.

"Whoever told you that was an idiot. Only weak men are intimated by strong women." He figured that should do it.

Felicity's eyes flashed. "There must have been some truth in it. This is what a typical night looks like for me, Chris. I'm alone."

He caught her hand and pressed it against his chest.

"Did I just become the invisible man or something? I'm here. So I think we can safely argue that you aren't alone."

"Simmons!"

Felicity felt a tug on the wire connected to her headset and heard Ed Bradshaw's bellow above the recorded interview she was listening to.

It was definitely Monday.

She turned off the tape recorder and smiled up at him. "Good morning, Mr. Bradshaw."

"It would be if Lyle hadn't called in sick. Says it's heatstroke but maybe if he'd stay off the golf course on the weekends he'd be at work today. Glenn is covering a charity baseball game tonight so that means you're going to the city council meeting. I already checked with Tim and he okayed it."

Felicity tried to keep a blank expression on her face, but inwardly she was singing a praise chorus. "I'll be there."

As Ed strode away, Felicity suddenly remembered that it was a Youth Connections night. Which meant Chris would be torn between two commitments—staying with her or going to Hickory Mills. The times overlapped, so it would be impossible for him to attend the council meeting and still have time to shoot some baskets.

Resisting the urge to call out to Ed and tell him she had plans for the evening, Felicity tapped her fingers impatiently against the keyboard. This was her job. She couldn't turn her back on the opportunity to cover the council meeting. Especially not when she was so close to wrapping up her feature.

Out of the five-piece spread that she'd recently pitched to Tim, she'd finished part three over the weekend. Now she needed a chance to talk to two of the city councilmen who teetered on the fence when it came to their stands on how they viewed community development. Usually the more heated debates within the council were hashed out during closed sessions, but Felicity had done enough research over the past two months to know who stood on which side. Or who sat in the middle. From past experience, she knew that if she applied some pressure, the fence sitters would shift their weight to the side they were leaning toward.

But what to do about Chris?

That, Felicity thought with a frown, was becoming the question of the day.

She was just getting used to spending her evening hours with him and suddenly, he'd invaded her weekends. Over the past two days, they'd spent a lot of time together around his work schedule.

Under any other circumstances—with anyone else—Felicity would have been miserable. But she was quickly learning that even though Chris was in her space, he never crowded her. Before he'd left on Friday evening, he'd asked her what her plans were for the weekend. She'd rattled off her short to-do list, which included working on her laptop, and when he'd shown up on Saturday, he was carrying a brown paper bag bulging with the ingredients for a homemade Italian dinner. While she sat at the table and worked on her article, he'd whipped up a batch of stuffed manicotti large enough to feed the neighborhood.

Sunday, at Chris's request, she'd attended the evening worship service at Northside Community instead of the one she usually attended in the morning. Pastor Abernathy obviously knew Chris well because he gave him a warm greeting when he saw them. In fact, *everyone* seemed to know him well. And he was definitely a kid magnet, too.

Whenever she looked, he had someone's child perched on his broad shoulder or tucked under his muscular arm.

Instead of resenting his presence, Felicity found herself…enjoying it.

She could get used to having him around.

No, she couldn't. Even though he'd talked her through a traumatic experience and offered her the comfort of his embrace afterward. Even though he made her laugh when he gave her a shoebox full of caramel candies. And even though he'd shaken her defenses when he'd bluntly stated his opinion of Lance, and other men who fell into the same category.

When she lay in bed that night, remembering Chris's response to what she'd shared, she realized it hadn't occurred to her that maybe Lance was the one who needed a lesson in character development. Somewhere deep inside herself, she'd accepted his words and began to believe them. And because she knew she couldn't force herself to become someone else, she accepted that she was probably going to be alone.

Until Chris had challenged her perception. Felicity had to admit that in the short time she'd known him, he'd already challenged her in a lot of ways. As a reporter, she'd met a lot of people but she'd never met anyone quite like Chris.

She had to remind herself that he'd only agreed to be her bodyguard to please his father and placate Tim. The source of the sparks that flew between them was the cross-purposes they found themselves in—Felicity knew that God was protecting her and Chris wanted to take over His job.

When she flipped open her phone to call Chris and tell him she was going to the city council meeting, she braced herself for more of those sparks.

"You seem a little distracted today, Chris." Nora reached over and ruffled his hair, just like she'd done hundreds of times while he was growing up.

"I'm all right," Chris said quickly. With all his mother had been going through, he hadn't told her much about Felicity, other than that someone had threatened her and he was staying close by when he wasn't on patrol.

Nora's brow furrowed. "It's your second job, isn't it? Keeping an eye on that reporter? You're getting worn out."

Chris smiled because she was fretting over him like he was still ten years old. "I'm only with Felicity until ten, Mom. I just feel bad because I'm not here at the hospital as often as I'd like to be."

Nora stirred a tiny container of creamer into her coffee, lost in thought. When she looked up at him, her eyes were moist. "Wallace should have been released almost two weeks ago. I can tell Dr. Strickland is concerned because your father is still so weak. He should be showing signs of improvement by now. He should be home."

Chris had done some Internet searches on bone marrow transplants and he knew what his mom was telling him lined up with what he'd been reading. "You made the right decision to keep him here," Chris assured her. "He's got round-the-clock medical care and until they pinpoint why he's not regaining his strength and where those low-grade fevers are coming from, this is the best place for him to be."

"Whenever your dad was sick in the past, I'd catch him sneaking out to go to the office for a few hours. I couldn't keep him down. But now…he's getting discouraged, Chris. I can feel it. Your dad's always had a hard time translating his love into words," Nora said softly. "He misses Jeremy and he's worried about Melissa. He won't ask, but he needs to know the rest of you are still here for him."

Chris wondered if maybe that was part of the reason Wallace was still so weak. Nora was right—his father did have a hard time verbalizing his feelings, especially when it came to his softer side. If he were being eaten up with guilt or worry, it would siphon off the energy necessary to speed up his recovery.

Chris frequently prayed that the Lord would draw Jeremy and Melissa back to the family, not just for his parents' sake but also for all of them. He was worried about Melissa, too, especially knowing that she'd left town with Dean Orton, a guy she'd met at a local club. Fortunately, he didn't have a criminal record but he was one of those musicians who lived a vagabond lifestyle so it was turning out to be difficult to discover where they'd gone. He didn't own a vehicle for Chris to trace and when he'd tracked down Dean's former roommate, all he could tell him was that Dean's band had a few gigs lined up.

"I'll talk to Dad," Chris promised his mother, silently questioning whether it would help. He discreetly glanced at his watch and saw that he still had another half an hour before Felicity was off work.

She'd left a cheerful message on his voice mail telling him that she had to work overtime so he could plan on going to Youth Connections without her that evening.

He assumed from the message that she'd be staying later at the newspaper, which meant that he could play basketball for an hour and then be there to pick her up when she was finished. He was torn, knowing that he needed to stay close to Felicity and wanting to be there for Pepper, who'd confided in him that his biological father had been hanging around lately because he'd gotten laid off from his job. The only trouble was,

Pepper's dad liked to hang around at the bars, too, and when he did it brought out the worst in him.

Nora linked her arm through his as they walked toward the elevator. When the door closed, Chris thought about Felicity. She'd tried hard to remain calm when she'd been trapped inside but it had obviously brought back a lot of bad memories. He remembered that vulnerable look in her eyes.

And the way she'd felt in his arms.

Chapter Thirteen

Felicity made sure she was at City Hall a few minutes before the meeting officially started. It was her way of gauging the political climate, which, depending on what was on the agenda, could be as chilly as the penguin exhibit at the zoo.

She lingered in the hallway, knowing from experience that some of the best conversations between the councilmen happened in the hallway. Shuffling through her things to find her tape recorder, Felicity pressed Play but there was a tiny click and nothing happened.

"Not dead batteries!" she groaned, rapping it on the palm of her hand, just in case it needed some inspiration.

Felicity stifled another groan. Punctuality was high on Mayor Whitmore's list of values and he called the meetings to order by the second hand on his watch.

There was a light on in one of the offices at the end of the hall and she decided to throw herself on the mercy of whoever was working late.

"Hello?" She rapped lightly on the door but couldn't see anyone inside the room.

Felicity glanced at her watch. She had two minutes to find batteries and get back to the meeting. Hoping she wouldn't be caught trespassing, she slipped into the office and picked a desk drawer. When she opened it, she found the treasure she was looking for.

Thank You, God! She popped the old batteries out and they bounced onto a thick stack of papers fanned out on the desk.

Blueprints.

She caught the batteries as they rolled over the words RiverMill Developers. River Bend Condominiums. The sketch under the title showed a row of brick luxury townhouses bordered by cobblestone sidewalks and old-fashioned lampposts. The river was in the foreground, winding in a peaceful ribbon not far from the front doorsteps.

There was no address and Felicity's curiosity got the best of her. But then her conscience kicked in. There were times when her obedience to God and His laws superseded her nosiness as a reporter! She stuck her hands in her pockets, just to keep them out of trouble for a moment, and fingers closed around her phone. Her camera phone. She snapped a photo of the sketch and gathered up her tape recorder, tossing the dead batteries into the wastebasket. Fifteen seconds to get back downstairs to the meeting.

Ernest Cromwell was just closing the door as she sprinted up to him.

"Excuse me," she said breathlessly.

He scowled but stepped to the side and let her pass. One of the reporters from the *Observer,* Perry Sharpe, grinned and tapped his watch meaningfully as she found an empty chair. They were the same age and covered the same beat but that was all they had in common. Perry loved to sensationalize the news and didn't want to be bothered by the facts unless he could twist them for his own purposes. As far as Felicity was concerned, he was working for the right newspaper.

She took notes during the first part of the meeting while several citizens voiced their complaints about garbage collection and then got her tape recorder ready for the second half of the session.

"Don't bother." Perry leaned over, so close that his breath stirred her hair. Felicity inched away. "While you were touching up your lipstick, Whitmore said they're going into closed session."

"About what?"

Perry simply shrugged. Which meant that either he knew and wasn't going to tell her or he didn't know and wanted to annoy her. She tamped down her frustration.

Ernest Cromwell cleared his throat as the hum of conversation over weekly garbage collection died down a bit. "We're moving into a closed session now, ladies and gentlemen. Mayor Whitmore will open the floor for five minutes to take your questions."

Felicity turned on her tape recorder and raised her hand. "Mayor Whitmore, you're on record as stating that community development means caring for the citizens of Davis Landing first. Did you know that a domestic-abuse shelter in Nashville was hoping to open a satellite shelter in Hickory Mills?"

As far as questions went, Felicity didn't think it would have the effect that it did. It was as if she'd lit the table in front of them on fire. Ever since Chris had mentioned the shelter, she'd wondered if Mayor Whitmore was really behind the things he claimed to be. In the feature she was writing, she wanted to give an unbiased portrayal of his stand on community development and to do that, she had to make sure his words lined up consistently with his actions.

Mayor Whitmore frowned at her and fiddled with the button on his vest. "No, I'm not aware of that."

Felicity's eyes widened. She wasn't as shocked that he had admitted it as she was that he hadn't known. Unease rippled through her. Was it possible that Chris had misinterpreted what the woman had told him?

"I think you've been misinformed, Miss Simmons," Ernest Cromwell interjected. "Or perhaps the Nashville shelter was simply making inquiries that didn't materialize into any action on their part. You aren't from the area and sometimes people like to 'bend the ear,' so to speak, of people who aren't familiar with an issue. Especially if it gets them on the front page of the newspaper."

Laughter rippled around the room and Felicity felt her face get warm. *You should know about wanting to make the front page,* she thought.

"I'm sorry we don't have time for any more questions," Mayor Whitmore said, still staring at Felicity.

"I'd like to thank everyone for coming. Thank you for your interest in—"

The future of Davis Landing, Felicity silently finished right along with him. Mayor Whitmore always closed the city council meetings with that pleasant little quip. In the past, it had sounded so sincere. Now she wasn't so sure.

"And you look down your cute little nose at the *Observer* for not getting our facts straight," Perry whispered, giving her a bold wink.

Felicity ignored him and scanned the faces around the table, hoping that the two councilmen she wanted to talk to would take a five-minute break. Unfortunately, her question must have riveted everyone to their chairs. No one wanted to risk being on the receiving end of her next question. Reluctantly, she gathered her things.

"Maybe if you just flash those big brown eyes at Mayor Whitmore he'll let you stay," Perry said as a parting shot.

Felicity ground her teeth together and fished in her pocket for a piece of candy. Thanks to Chris, she now had a year's supply. Or maybe a *month's* supply, depending on how many times the council convened for closed sessions!

She'd walked to the courthouse from Hamilton Media, knowing it would still be light outside when she left. It was only eight o'clock. If she hurried, she'd be back to the *Dispatch* before Chris left Youth Connections. Guilt tapped at her conscience and she brushed it away. She'd told him the truth when she'd said she was working overtime…she just hadn't told him she was covering a meeting. And once she was back safe and sound, it wouldn't be worth mentioning again. Hopefully.

The heat had pushed everyone indoors for the evening so there weren't many people on the street as Felicity unlocked the door to the side entrance. When Chris found her, she'd be sitting at her desk typing up her notes from the meeting.

She pushed open the door and a tall shape loomed in front of her.

"Overtime, huh?"

Felicity pressed a hand against her heart and laughed weakly. "I thought you were supposed to be watching out for me, not scaring me to death."

"It would be easier to watch you if I knew where you were."

Felicity met his gaze but Chris saw the flicker of guilt in her eyes and somehow it made him feel better.

"You just forgot to tell me that it wouldn't be *here*." He nodded, anchoring his hands on his hips. "I should have known better than to trust you."

"You can trust me," Felicity said, shocked that he'd even say such a thing. "But Ed gave me back my city council meeting—by default, but still—and I was only a block away. I wasn't alone."

"Lie of omission."

She gasped. "No, it's not."

Chris bit the inside of his cheek to keep from smiling. "You sound a little defensive, Scoop."

"I'm just going to drop some things off at my desk and then you can escort me home, Officer Hamilton."

"Not so fast." Chris put his hand on her arm and felt the same jolt of electricity he'd felt when he'd put her hand against his chest. Like someone had just used a portable defibrillator on him. "Come with me."

"To the interrogation room?" Felicity said under her breath.

Now he did smile. She looked so defiant and so…sorry. She *should* be sorry, he told himself. She made his job more difficult whenever she stepped out on her own. When he'd gotten to the *Dispatch* and realized she wasn't in the building, he'd immediately called Tim, who knew she was covering the city council meeting but assumed Chris was with her. After allowing his big brother to chew him out for a few minutes, he was about to go and find her when he'd heard the key in the door.

"No interrogation. A simple lesson in the buddy system. Something that's a foreign concept to you." Chris turned on the light in the front lobby and watched as Felicity scoped out the area. And came to rest on the stairwell, which had yellow police tape stretched across it.

"What's that for?" she asked suspiciously.

"You can't cross it." Chris shrugged and bumped her toward the elevator. "Your mission, should you choose to accept it, is to go to the third floor of Hamilton Media."

Felicity's feet stopped moving. It was only his hand pressed into the small of her back that propelled her forward. "Chris—"

"You've heard that old saying that if you fall off a horse you're supposed to get right back on, haven't you?"

"I like horses. I don't like enclosed spaces."

"And when you finally forced yourself to face your fear, it backfired and probably made it worse. You said that you hated small spaces but hated that you hated them even more, remember?"

"I—" She remembered.

"Time to get back in the saddle."

"You said this was going to be a lesson in the *buddy* system!"

"It is. You ride the elevator and I cheer you on." He urged her to the door and pressed the button. When it opened, he felt her entire body stiffen. Compassion welled up inside him as she bravely stepped inside. The eyes that locked onto his were dark with anxiety when she realized he was making her go alone.

"You can do this, Felicity. And just to give you an incentive, there'll be something special waiting for you on the third floor."

"What?"

He grinned. "Me."

The door closed and Felicity instinctively took a step back. When she looked at the panel, she saw that Chris had pressed every single button. Which meant that she was going to stop at every floor. Okay, there were only two of them, but still…

The elevator stopped on two and the door opened. Chris was standing there, gasping for breath. "Piece of cake, Scoop. You're doing great."

The door closed. Felicity started to laugh. She was still laughing when the elevator stopped on three and the door opened again.

Chris was there, holding out his hand. Without hesitating, she reached out and grabbed it.

And pulled him inside.

Felicity felt her heart pounding but this time it wasn't from anxiety. Chris's eyes were soft. Knowing.

"Thanks," she murmured, suddenly overwhelmed.

"You don't have to go through everything alone, Scoop." He laced his fingers through hers and she could feel the gentle strength in his hand.

"I don't. I always rely on God." She did. One of God's promises was to be with her wherever she went and she believed it with all her heart. That was one of the points of conflict between her and Chris. When she'd been trapped in the elevator, she'd asked God to strengthen her...

And then she'd heard Chris's voice.

Her breath caught.

"I rely on God, too, but we're a body of believers because He wants us to be interdependent." Chris gazed at her intently. "Leaning on someone doesn't mean that you don't trust God...or that you're weak. I think it just means you're human. The bottom line is, we're bearing each other's burdens and that's something God wants us to do, too."

That the elevator had stopped again barely registered with Felicity. Chris was right. For years she'd had to prove her mettle as a reporter by being tough and assertive. Maybe she had gone to an extreme—feeling as if any sign of vulnerability would be viewed as a weakness, would mean that she wasn't capable. It had subtly leaked into other areas of her life—even her spiritual life—and she hadn't realized it until now. Maybe when she'd asked God to strengthen her, He wanted to teach her something.

That sometimes He strengthened His people…by providing people.

Chapter Fourteen

By the end of the next day, Felicity felt she had a bruise on her forehead from running into brick walls. After the third frustratingly brief conversation she'd had with people she hoped would know something about the RiverMill condos, she wasn't ready to quit. Something was going on. She could feel it. As if someone had dropped a puzzle at her feet, she tried to pick up the pieces and make sense out of them. The more people refused to talk, the more convinced Felicity was that there was something they weren't supposed to talk about. She was ready to work all night.

Except that Chris would be coming to pick her up and take her to Hickory Mills. The heat wave had released Davis Landing from its clutches so he and Jason had scheduled an extra game for the boys that evening. The men's Bible study at Northside had offered to treat everyone to ice cream sundaes afterward. On the way home the night before, after Chris had run her through the faith-building-by-elevator training course, he'd told her about the trouble Pepper was having at home. He'd also mentioned that the boys were disappointed she hadn't come with him, which arrowed straight to her heart. She'd only spent one evening with them and it had impacted her in a way she hadn't thought it would. No wonder Chris and Jason devoted so much time to the kids.

Felicity sighed. There was the point of contention. She only had so much time and her career had a tendency to crowd other things out.

Maybe because you let it.

The quiet words resonated in her thoughts and for once she let herself dwell on them instead of chasing them away. She'd always told herself that making her career a priority would prove her determination and dedication. If she gave one hundred and ten percent to proving she was a serious reporter, she could restore some balance to her life when her career was solidly established. That had been her motto for eight years— why was she questioning it now?

Felicity's fingers tapped against the stack of papers on her desk. Ordinarily she would have worked through the night if it meant she'd have a great article ready by the next deadline. The trail she was following could get cold if she didn't press forward.

So why was she willing—even looking forward to— spending her evening playing basketball instead of finding out if the mayor was up to the buttons on his plaid vest in lies? It didn't make any sense. Why was she losing her focus?

"Ready to go?" Chris poked his head around the wall of her cubicle and Felicity's toes curled in her shoes. Every time she saw him, her heart reacted like she was staring at the biggest present under the Christmas tree.

Maybe *that* was the reason she was losing her focus.

Chris saw the inward struggle reflected in her eyes. The papers spread out on her desk, the open phone book at her elbow and the text still filling her computer screen clearly told him that she wasn't ready to leave work.

He hadn't realized he was holding his breath until Felicity nodded. She reached down to grab a canvas bag near her feet, but her movements were slow, as if she still wasn't sure she wanted to leave.

"Judging from the mountain of papers on your desk, it looks like you've had a busy day."

She tilted her head, regarding him so intently that he was tempted to cross his eyes, just to make her laugh. "I was working on my feature. I may have hit a big snag so I've been trying to unravel it to find out what it is and where it started."

When Chris had spent time with Felicity over the weekend, she'd mentioned the feature she'd been quietly devoting her off hours to. Even though it hadn't been formally assigned, she confided in him that she hoped it would be the springboard to a weekly political column.

Chris exhaled slowly. "The men's Bible study group is going to be at Y.C. tonight—I'm sure they can get along without me for the evening. I'll just hang out here in the lobby until you're finished working. Maybe ride up and down on the elevator a few times." He winked at her.

Felicity froze, her eyes searching his face. Looking for…what? Chris wasn't sure. She shrugged the bag onto her shoulder and her next words catapulted him into left field. "They may be able to get along without *you* tonight but I doubt my team can get along without me. The snag will still be there tomorrow. Let's go."

A few hours later, Chris realized he was seeing God at work again. Only this time He was using Felicity. Pepper's older sister and several of her friends had heard about the ice cream sundaes and had wandered into the gym during the last quarter of the game. Most of the boys' focus dissolved like sugar in water at the sight of bare midriffs and shorts.

Chris's first response was to shoo the girls away but Felicity had immediately jogged over to them and started up a conversation. Within minutes, basking in the glow of Felicity's attention, their bored expressions became animated and they looked more like the young girls they were instead of miniature pop stars.

Now they were all huddled together in a corner, eating ice cream and giggling. And Felicity was right in the middle of it. He wondered if she realized that the confidence and independence she projected—the qualities she claimed that men shied away from—were the ones that drew people to her?

The girls in the neighborhood needed someone like Felicity to mentor them. Even with three sisters, he didn't pretend to understand the inner workings of the female mind, but it was obvious that Felicity did.

Lord, You brought Felicity and these girls here tonight for a reason. I know she devotes a lot of time to her career but she had the chance to stay and work later tonight and she came here instead. If You want Felicity to be involved with this ministry, You'll have to be the one to open her heart to the needs here.

It was a good thing he made a habit of praying with his eyes open because he saw the basketball sail through the air like an orange missile. The boy who'd lost control of it temporarily lost the ability to speak, too, because he was frozen in place as he and the rest of the boys tracked its course to Felicity and the small cluster of girls that surrounded her.

Chris didn't even have time to yell out a "head's up." But he didn't have to. In one graceful motion, Felicity put herself between the ball and the girls and caught it with one hand a split second before it hit anyone.

There was a supercharged moment of silence and then the girls squealed, circling Felicity like the colorful charms on her bracelet.

"Can you teach us how to do that?" he heard one of them ask above the commotion. "The boys always brag they can beat us."

Over the girls' heads, Felicity's gaze met his. Her hair was mussed from the game they'd just finished playing, her clothes damp and crumpled from the crush of girls as they eagerly crowded around her. Chris held his breath, the prayer he'd just said still lingering near the edges of his memory.

"What do you think, Officer Hamilton?" she called out. "Do you think my girls can have some floor time during the week?"

My girls. Chris's throat closed without warning. Felicity wasn't the kind of person who could be backed into a corner. If she were volunteering to coach the girls, she'd do it only because she *wanted* to. Or because God was calling her to.

Don't get all soggy now, Hamilton.

"I think we can work something out," he said, deliberately nonchalant.

Felicity's expression told him that his casual tone wasn't fooling her for a minute. How was it that in such a short time they could read each other so well?

Jason's whistle pierced through the buzz of the kids' conversation. "Okay, listen up, guys. And girls. Time to wrap it up for the night. Chris, you got a minute?" Jason jerked his head toward the tiny room they used to store the sports equipment.

Chris followed him inside and was surprised when Jason closed the door. "What's up?"

"This." Jason sighed the word and handed Chris an envelope. "It was in the mailbox when I got here tonight."

Chris pulled out a plain sheet of white paper with a brief message typed on it.

Dear Youth Connections Committee,

After considering your recent request to purchase the buildings on 24 River Street in Hickory Mills, I am writing to inform you that I have decided not to sell at this time. Furthermore, it is with much regret that, due to unforeseen circumstances, I will be unable to continue to rent out the afore-mentioned property. I will, however, give you until the first week of September to vacate the premises of any equipment, personal items, etc. After that, all remaining property will be considered abandoned and will be disposed of.

Roland Sykes

Chris had to skim the letter again, just to make sure he'd read it right the first time. "He's not only backing out on the sale but now they're refusing to let us rent the building?"

Jason's expression was grim. "It looks that way."

"I don't get it. We offered him a fair price for three empty, dilapidated buildings that the pigeons don't even want to live in. What happened?"

"I have no idea," Jason said quietly, as frustrated and upset as Chris was.

"I'll call Mr. Sykes in the morning and talk to him. Something isn't right. I can understand not selling, but why won't he let us continue to rent?"

Jason shrugged helplessly and plowed his fingers through his hair. "I don't think we should say anything to the kids yet. We've got a few weeks to talk to the committee and pray about what to do next. God has a big mountain to move because I can't think of any place else that will fit our needs. Or our budget."

Chris silently agreed. The property on River Street was located right where the need was greatest. Most of the boys walked to Youth Connections. If they had to rely on their parents for transportation to another part of town, Chris could guarantee that the size of their weekly group would be cut in half.

Discouragement washed over him as he folded the letter. "I'll see you back at the apartment. I have to take Felicity home."

"Sure. I'll make sure everything is locked up."

Felicity knew the second she saw Chris's face that something bad had happened. If it hadn't been for the shadows in his eyes, his forced smile was a dead giveaway. She wondered if it had something to do with Pepper or one of the other boys.

When Chris dropped her off at home, he always walked her to the front door but now he simply cut the engine and waited for her to get off the motorcycle.

Felicity hesitated. She didn't want to pry but then she remembered a certain exercise involving police tape on the stairs and an elevator. Maybe it was time to return the favor. "What's wrong, Chris?"

He gave her a wry glance. "My game face isn't on?"

Maybe to anyone else, Felicity thought, *but not to me.* "You don't have to go through things alone. The buddy system, remember?"

Chris winced at the reminder. "I got a letter tonight

from Mr. Sykes, who owns the building where Youth Connections meets. He's decided not to sell."

"Oh, no." Felicity couldn't believe it. "Did he say why?"

"Unforeseen circumstances or something like that. But there's more. He doesn't want to rent us the space, either. After the first week of September, we have to close the doors." Chris's voice was ragged and automatically Felicity reached out and took his hand.

"I'm sorry." It was worse than she thought. A sudden suspicion crept in. This was exactly what Chris had told her had happened with the director of the domestic-abuse shelter. What had he said? Two days before the sale, the owner of the building had backed out? In the same neighborhood.

The blueprints for the RiverMill Development condominiums flashed through her mind.

"All I can think of is how hard it's going to be to find another building. To rent or to buy. If we relocate, we might lose some of the kids—"

"Wait a second," Felicity interrupted, distracted by the discouragement in Chris's voice. "This is God's ministry and He's going to watch out for it, right? It isn't up to you to shoulder the whole burden."

Chris's lips twisted. "I may have a tendency to do that."

The admission was meek but the glint of humor in his eyes told Felicity that her comment had hit home. Then she became aware of his thumb brushing against her palm in a gentle sweeping motion. She swallowed hard. What was that silly expression? *Weak in the knees?* She suddenly knew what it meant. And what it felt like.

"We're quite a pair, aren't we, Scoop?" Chris murmured.

"Because you want to save the world and I want to write about it?" She tried to pass off his comment with a laugh but instead her voice sounded…breathless. *Wait a second,* she thought wildly, *I want a do over!*

"No, because it drives us crazy if we can't handle something on our own."

What was he talking about? That may have described her internal code but she didn't think it described Chris. In spite of the trials the Hamiltons were facing, he had a close family. He had a best friend who'd take a bullet for him and a bunch of kids who respected him. His faith was well grounded, rooted in a sincere love for God. He was connected to people in a way that she hadn't allowed herself to be.

She gently disengaged her hand from his because it was easier to think when the warmth of his thumb wasn't branding her skin. "It looks to me like you know when to call in for reinforcements. Who taught me about the buddy system?" she reminded him.

"You actually listened to me for once?"

"Saved in the 'words of wisdom' file. Right next to one from my mom that says don't use a dish towel to take a pan of chocolate chip cookies out of the oven."

Chris slid his hands into the front pockets of his jeans. "The buddy system, hmm? Does that mean you're going to help me find a new place for Youth Connections?"

"I'll help you. You're going to be happy that you're stuck with a nosy reporter."

Then her heart missed a beat when she heard him say something under his breath that sounded suspiciously like, "I already am."

Lying in bed later that night, she convinced herself she'd imagined it.

Chapter Fifteen

"You look like you just lost your best friend," Stella said as she came into the kitchen and spotted Felicity, who was slumped at the table in her pajamas, drowning her cornflakes with the back of a spoon.

Maybe she had.

Felicity shook the thought away as quickly as it surfaced. The day before, Tim finally decided he agreed with her about the threats, so he'd officially fired her bodyguard. She hadn't known until Chris had stopped by the *Dispatch* to tell her the news. And he didn't look a bit happy with Tim's decision.

What shocked Felicity was that *she* wasn't as happy with Tim's decision as she thought she'd be! Maybe that had something to do with the subtle change in her and Chris's relationship over the course of the week. The change that had left Felicity feeling off balance, wondering what was going to happen next. There had been times when she'd felt the weight of his gaze resting on her, but it didn't make her uncomfortable. Just the opposite. It had somehow made her feel more…secure.

When she'd heard footsteps and looked up to see Chris standing next to her cubicle, she could tell by the rigid set of his shoulders that something was wrong. In a curt tone, Chris had told her that Tim had just met him in the lobby and informed him he was no longer "needed." His eyes blamed her and even though she tried to explain that Tim hadn't warned her, either, she wasn't sure Chris believed her. After all, she was the one who'd told him if she hadn't received any more letters or threats by the end of the week, she was going to ask Tim to fire him.

After Chris left, Felicity felt the loss of his presence in unexpected ways. She'd picked out a video for the evening with him in mind but instead she'd watched it by herself, wondering if he was at the hospital with his family, happy that he was back in his routine again instead of babysitting her. When her Friday night routine had begun to include Chris, she realized she'd started looking forward to the weekend instead of viewing it simply as a two-day hurdle to jump so she could dive into work on Monday.

"It's a good thing that Chris feels the threats have stopped, right?" Stella poured herself a cup of coffee and sat down at the table across from Felicity. "You can go back to life as usual. And I can put my trellis back up."

Life as usual. Why did that seem so depressing all

of a sudden? "I think I'll go down to the *Dispatch* and work for a few hours," Felicity said, cringing when she saw what she'd done to an innocent bowl of cereal.

Just because she and Chris weren't stuck together anymore didn't mean she'd abandon him...or, she quickly amended, her search for answers about the sale of the buildings on River Street. So far her attempts had been as futile as the ones she'd made that week to contact Wes Greene about the River Bend condos. Her next plan—which she was going to carry out on Monday—was to camp out in his office until he agreed to meet with her.

"We could see a movie tonight," Stella offered. "Actually *go* to one instead of renting it."

"That might be fun." *Snap out of your blue mood, girl!* "I should be back in a few hours."

"It's Saturday," Stella reminded her. "I'm calling you if you aren't home by supper."

"Yes, Mother." Felicity rolled her eyes.

Since the *Dispatch* put out its weekend edition on Friday, the offices were quiet on Saturday. Ordinarily she looked forward to working in a setting where the phones weren't ringing constantly and Tim wasn't prowling around, putting everyone on edge.

She pulled up her notes on the computer and a colorful pop up ad for a dating service suddenly invaded her screen.

Tired of being alone on Friday night?

"Oh, please!" She deleted it and tried to concentrate

on the information she was compiling for her feature, but all her brain wanted to assimilate was Chris. His smile. The way his eyes warmed like melted toffee when he teased her. The funny, impromptu cheerleading pose he'd struck—which he'd probably learned from his sisters—when the elevator door had opened on the second floor that night....

She finally admitted defeat and went home.

Stella was putting the finishing touches on a salad when Felicity came into the kitchen. "Wow. This is a record for you—you were only gone an hour. You must have been inspired."

Inspired, no. Totally distracted, yes.

"Or maybe you smelled the flowers all the way downtown?"

"Flowers?"

"You didn't notice the florist box that's taking up most of the sofa? It came for you not long after you left. I promise I didn't open it up and take a peek—although I admit I was tempted."

Felicity headed back into the living room with Stella at her heels. The slim white box was tied with a beautiful red satin bow and Felicity's mouth went dry. Maybe Chris had been thinking about her, too.

"Aren't you going to open it? I've had to wait an hour to see what's inside. And who they're from," Stella added, although her mischievous smile told Felicity she'd already guessed who'd sent them.

Felicity untied the bow and lifted the top. She wrinkled her nose as a sweet, cloying fragrance wafted up from the contents. She heard Stella's gasp before she realized what she was looking at. The flowers in the box—a dozen roses—were dead. The petals were dry and crisp; the thorn-spiked stems a dark brown.

With shaking fingers, Felicity picked up the card that was tucked in between the stems.

You Were Warned. Now You're Dead.

"Felicity!" Stella clutched her arm.

"Who delivered these?" Felicity asked, unable to tear her gaze away from the words on the card.

"A teenage boy," Stella whispered. "I assumed he was from the floral place on Main Street. I didn't pay much attention to him. He said your name…that the flowers were for Felicity Simmons."

Felicity dropped the card into the box, her fingers trembling. This had to be someone's idea of a sick joke.

"Felicity?" Stella drew a ragged breath. "He knows where you—where we—live."

Seventy-five. Seventy-six.

Chris wondered how many push-ups it was going to take to purge Felicity Simmons from his thoughts. Maybe he'd have to run a few miles, too. He'd spent the morning at the hospital and Heather had quickly picked up on the fact that he wasn't himself. All Chris knew was that it was a good thing Tim wasn't there. After overriding his opinion about staying close to Felicity, his older brother wasn't exactly the "sibling of the week."

The telephone rang and Chris decided to ignore it.

"Chris? Are you there?"

He heard Felicity's voice on the answering machine and dove for the phone.

"Felicity? Sorry about that," he panted. "I'm here."

"A bouquet of roses was delivered a while ago," she said. "They're, uh…dead."

"Dead?" Chris rubbed the back of his neck, assuming he hadn't heard her right.

"Dead." She paused. "There was a note with them."

Chris's hand clenched around the phone as he realized what she was telling him. "What did it say?"

Felicity repeated the message softly but Chris heard the thread of fear in her voice, which opened up the floodgate of adrenaline that rushed through him.

"Did you get the flowers at home or at work?"

"At home. I was at the *Dispatch* but Stella was here."

"How long ago?" Chris anchored the telephone between his ear and his shoulder and yanked his shoes on.

"An hour."

"Lock the doors and windows. I'll be right over." *Lord, keep them safe.* "Don't let anyone in."

He slipped a shoulder holster on, took his gun out of its case, punched the clip in the bottom and jammed it into the holster. On his way out the door, he yanked a sweatshirt jacket off the hook and pulled it on. His heart rate matched his pace as he sprinted to the garage and opted for his car instead of his motorcycle.

When he reached the apartment, Felicity met him at

the front door, her eyes wide and her skin stripped of color. Stella stood several feet behind her, her hands nervously twisting her shirttail.

"The roses are on the sofa," Felicity said evenly. "I touched the note, so it probably has my fingerprints all over it."

She was trying to be calm but he picked up the tremor in her voice. Chris felt a surge of frustration. What was he? A cop? A bodyguard? A friend? Chris realized it didn't matter at the moment. Not when Felicity looked as brittle as the flowers lying in the box. He reached out and took her hand, giving it a comforting squeeze. They could figure out the changing rules of their relationship when she was in a safe place.

"Neither of you can stay here tonight," Chris said, feeling Felicity's fingers tighten in his. "Pack an overnight bag. I'm going to take you both somewhere safe until we figure out our next step."

Stella nodded and headed toward her bedroom, but Felicity didn't move. Her gaze was riveted on the roses. Chris flipped the top of the box over them.

"Go on, Felicity," he urged quietly. "Let's get you out of here."

Her eyes were shadowed when she looked up at him, but she forced a smile. "Aren't you going to say 'I told you so'?"

"I make it a rule to only use that phrase when it comes to my brothers and sisters," Chris said with a wink, matching her attempt at normalcy. He gave her a gentle nudge toward the doorway. "Just for the record, though, I'm not leaving your side until I find out who sent them."

To his amazement, Felicity didn't argue. When she disappeared into her bedroom to pack, Chris exhaled slowly to regain his focus. He noticed right away that the card wasn't stamped with a florist's logo and it had been handwritten. The penmanship was large and sloppy, as if someone under extreme stress had written it. Almost two weeks had gone by with no contact from the stalker, and now this.

A cold knot formed in Chris's stomach as he looked at the flowers. Whoever sent the flowers had a flair for the dramatic. The sickly sweet scent that attacked his nostrils had obviously been sprayed on the roses.

Chris carefully picked up the bouquet to see if there was anything else in the box, and his next breath stalled when he realized that instead of tissue paper, the flowers were nestled in Friday's edition of the *Dispatch*.

All these little details added together created the big picture. It hadn't been enough to let Felicity know that her safety was at risk. Whoever had sent the roses wanted her to know that she wasn't safe at *home* now, either.

He walked over to the phone and called Jason, who'd taken several of the boys from Youth Connections out for hamburgers. When he'd explained what had happened and the need to continue to keep the situation quiet for his family's sake, Jason offered to come over and gather the evidence while Chris took Stella and Felicity to a safe house.

"I've got a key to Jeremy's apartment—he's out of town for a few days," Chris told his partner. "I'll take them there."

"Good idea," Jason said. "The boys and I are done eating now so I'll be right over."

Chris hung up the phone, feeling the knot inside him ease slightly. He wouldn't feel completely settled until Felicity and Stella were safely tucked away. He only hoped if his brother came home unexpectedly, he wouldn't mind finding some uninvited guests.

Felicity emerged from the bedroom with a small overnight bag in one hand and her laptop case in the other.

"Ready?" Chris didn't want to tell her where he was taking them yet.

"I'm taking Sushi."

Her clown fish. He glanced at the saltwater aquarium that was large enough to accommodate a school of tuna. "Do we have to—" He saw her expression and sighed. "Where's the net?"

Felicity stared up at the ceiling in Jeremy Hamilton's guest room, unable to sleep. If she closed her eyes, all she could see was the bouquet of dead roses. Then her imagination took over, coming up with one grim scenario after another. In the darkness, problems seemed larger than life. The Scripture verses she could readily call upon during the day were now frozen in her internal hard drive.

Stella tossed restlessly in the twin bed on the other side of the room and Felicity felt guilt pressing down on her. In her stubborn refusal to listen to Chris's warning that she might still be at risk, she hadn't considered that she might be dragging her best friend directly into the line of fire, too.

The minutes turned into hours and each one dragged by. She'd seen Chris toss a blanket and pillow on Jeremy's couch but somehow she knew he wasn't sleeping, either. Finally, as daylight slipped under the shade, she heard his quiet movements in the kitchen.

"Hi." She came around the corner and knew her theory was right. He hadn't slept, either, most likely by choice. His shirt was untucked but he was still wearing his shoulder holster and she could see the butt of his gun jutting out of it. Dark stubble shadowed the bottom half of his face but his eyes were clear and alert.

"Morning." His voice came out in a rough purr as he turned and poured another cup of coffee.

Felicity skimmed her hands through her hair and realized that it was loose around her shoulders. Self-consciously she pushed it away from her face and sat down at the table. "I'd like to go to church this morning."

Chris frowned. "I don't think that's a good idea—"

"I need to," Felicity interrupted. "Please, Chris. I know I can't go home but I can't hide in this apartment, either. If fear keeps me from worshipping God, then he's won."

"Felicity's right," Stella said sleepily from the doorway. "Count me in."

"All right. But prepare yourself to be interrogated by the best."

"Interrogated?" Felicity frowned.

Chris's lips tilted. "My mom and my sisters go to the first service."

Felicity had seen Nora Hamilton in passing and had even met her briefly at a church function, but when she stepped into the sanctuary with Chris at her side, she knew that Chris's mom was suddenly looking at her in a whole new light. So were Amy and Heather, even though both of them had to know that the only reason Chris was with her was because he'd been hired to be.

Since she, Stella and Chris had slipped in just as the prelude was starting, they didn't have a chance to talk to Chris's family until the service ended. Stella hurried away to talk to some friends and Felicity watched Nora make her way over to them, struck again by how beautiful Chris's mother was. With her petite frame and delicate, youthful features, she could have easily been mistaken for one of the Hamilton sisters.

"Chris! You should have told me you were coming to the early service. We would have saved a place for you." Nora embraced her son and then her wide-spaced hazel eyes settled on Felicity. "You must be Miss Simmons. Chris has told me about you."

Felicity's eyes narrowed at Chris and he gave her an innocent shrug.

"It's nice to see you again, Mrs. Hamilton."

"Please, call me Nora. I'm sure you've met Amy and Heather." Nora stepped back and once again Felicity felt herself being weighed and measured, this time by Chris's sisters.

Amy was dressed much the same for church as she dressed for work, with her golden-blond hair in a fashionable style and her blue eyes friendly but curious. Heather had an appealing smile and her eyes were the same shade of brown as Chris's. Her hair was several shades lighter than her brother's, glowing softly with russet highlights.

"We've run into each other on occasion," Heather said.

"Trying to get away from Tim, no doubt," the man standing beside her murmured, his dark eyes sparkling with amusement. Heather shushed him and gave Felicity an apologetic look. "You've met Ethan Danes?" Her cheeks tinted with pink as *Nashville Living*'s staff photographer dropped a casual kiss on top of her head.

Felicity felt a twinge of envy at the look that passed between them and she nodded. Occasionally Ethan did some work for the *Dispatch,* too, if their own photographer wasn't available.

"We're going out for brunch and then over to the hospital," Nora said. "Would you two like to join us?"

"Maybe another time, Mom," Chris said. "I'll stop by later this afternoon to check on Dad, though."

Nora flashed a warm smile at Felicity. "I hope to see you again, Felicity."

Amy and Heather both joined in that chorus and Felicity felt her face grow warm. Until she noticed that Chris looked as uncomfortable as she felt.

"I've got to talk to Stella," Felicity murmured after Chris's family was out of earshot. "She's nervous about going back to the apartment today."

"She shouldn't. And neither should you—"

"I *live* there," Felicity said. "You don't know when Jeremy is going to come back and I'm sure that under the circumstances, he isn't going to want strangers hanging around."

"We'll have to come up with an alternate plan, then, because I'm not letting you go home."

"You're not *letting* me?"

A gentle cough distracted them both. Felicity glanced up to see Stella and Dawn Leroux standing a few feet away from them, watching her and Chris's exchange with fascination. On Stella's right were two dark-haired young girls who were giggling softly. They closely resembled the young woman positioned directly behind them, studying an invisible spot on the ceiling.

"Felicity, I have to agree with Chris on this," Stella said quietly. "Neither one of us should go back to the apartment yet. Chris, you know my friend Gabriela Valencia, don't you? She's offered to let me stay with her and the girls for a few days."

The pretty dark-haired woman extended her hand to Felicity and then to Chris. "It's Gabi. The only time I hear Gabriela is when my mother is upset with me," she said, her lighthearted tone easing the tension in the air. "These are my daughters, Veronica and Talia."

"Are you going to stay with us, too?" Talia, the younger of the two girls, asked Felicity cheerfully.

"No, I'm going to—"

"Stay with my sister and my mom." Chris finished her sentence and Felicity's mouth fell open.

"That's great." Stella couldn't hide her relief. "I was praying that God would provide a safe place for you."

Stella's heartfelt words sucked the fight right out of Felicity. She hadn't forgotten the lesson God had imprinted on her heart in the elevator that night but she hadn't expected to have to put it into practice so soon! God was showing her that He was protecting her. But He was doing things His way. Again!

She inwardly sighed, willing to consider the fact that if Stella had prayed, maybe God had provided Chris's childhood home as the answer.

Chapter Sixteen

The more Chris thought about it, the more he realized how practical his suggestion was. The Hamilton house may have been built at the turn of the century but it boasted a state-of-the-art security system and Felicity wouldn't be alone. Even if Heather or Nora were at the hospital, their housekeeper, Vera Mae, would be close by and nothing escaped her notice.

Chris had taken Stella and Felicity back to the apartment one more time so they could pack the additional things they'd need for a lengthier stay somewhere else. He could sense Felicity's struggle—she didn't want to stay in a place that might not be safe but she didn't want it to look like she was running away, either.

"Are you sure your mother and Heather won't mind having a stranger dropped on their doorstep?" Felicity asked, breaking the silence that had fallen between them as they drove through Davis Landing and past the city limits.

"I think we can find a better place for you than the doorstep," Chris said lightly. "Maybe the closet under the stairs."

Felicity didn't smile. "I'm serious, Chris. I don't want to be a burden. Your family is going through enough right now without feeling like they have an audience."

"I already called them while you were packing. Heather really misses Melissa and she sounded excited about having you there. To tell you the truth, it might be good for them. Especially Mom. She loves company."

"What if my being there puts them at risk? I should just stay at a hotel for a few days."

Chris wanted to beat his forehead against the steering wheel. *Come on, Scoop, work with me here.* "Believe me, if I thought there was the slightest chance I was putting you and my family at risk, I'd go with another plan. This is the best way, Felicity. Trust me."

Trust me.

Those two simple words decimated the walls that Felicity was trying to build. Hot tears scratched at the back of her eyes. Anger welled up inside her—not at Chris but at the anonymous person who'd turned her life completely inside out in the past twenty-four hours. Because of him, she had to leave her home. Rely on the goodwill of people she didn't know.

Lord, I know You don't want me to be overcome by fear, or doubt. Nothing that's happening is a surprise to You.

Chris's fingers suddenly closed around hers and Felicity's prayer connected to the man sitting beside her. No, the things that had happened *weren't* a surprise to God. She did trust God's protection but it was stretching her mind around the fact that maybe…just maybe…the promise of His protection had been answered this time in the strong, solid shape of her bodyguard. The same man she couldn't stop thinking about.

"Mom wants to put you in one of the guest rooms on third floor," Heather said, bumping Chris out of the way with her hip and looping her arm through Felicity's. She'd met them at the front door and immediately appointed herself the official tour guide.

And Felicity needed one. She tried not to stare at the massive crystal chandelier positioned above them as they walked into the front entryway. She knew the Hamiltons were one of the wealthiest families in the area but she hadn't realized that Chris's childhood home would be an enormous Greek Revival-style mansion that could have graced the cover of an issue of *Nashville Living* itself.

"That's the banister that Chris used to slide down," Heather said, pointing to the sweeping staircase that showcased the far end of the foyer. "Three stitches, right, Chris?"

"Four."

"He was kind of accident-prone when he was little," she said to Felicity in a stage whisper.

"I was not." Chris pretended to bristle but his eyes sparkled with affection for his sister. "If you remember, I got the stitches when *you* slid down the banister. I tried to catch you but Vera Mae had just polished it that day so you shot down like a tiny missile."

"Right. And I launched him head first into the antique side table over there." Heather laughed and reached out a hand to muss her brother's hair. "He was always in rescue mode. No wonder he decided to make it a career."

Chris rolled his eyes. "You're taking credit for that now?"

Felicity listened to their teasing banter and recognized Heather's attempts to put her at ease. Once she'd gotten over the initial shock of her first impression of Nora and Wallace's house, a closer look had revealed that it wasn't a museum…it was a *home*. Chris hadn't just lived in it—he'd grown up in it. Chased after his sisters on the gleaming hardwood floors. Probably played hide-and-seek with his brothers and had a hundred spots to choose from.

"Why don't you get Felicity's suitcase out of the car and I'll show her the guest room," Heather suggested. "Mom put her in the green room."

"I'll leave you two alone only if you promise you won't bore Felicity with any more stories."

"I'm a reporter. I love stories," Felicity said, earning an approving nod from Chris's twin.

"Right." Chris sighed and headed back toward the leaded-glass front door.

Heather chuckled softly but then her expression

turned serious. "Chris told me about the flowers and the message, Felicity. I can't believe someone could be so malicious. Mom and I are both glad you took Chris up on his offer to stay with us for a few days."

"It wasn't exactly an offer," Felicity admitted wryly.

Heather smiled. "I can imagine. He teases Tim for being stubborn but I have to admit it's in the Hamilton genes. He takes his job very seriously."

Felicity knew he took his job seriously, but was that all she was? Remembering the times over the past week when she'd felt that tingling connection dance between them, she wondered if he'd felt it, too. It was hard to separate the man from the job—Heather's loving insight into his personality confirmed that. God had hardwired Chris with a desire to protect people and she just happened to be one of them.

But is that enough for you?

The question came out of nowhere and blindsided Felicity. She slumped into a floral chintz chair by the window, vaguely aware that Heather was reminiscing about Chris's aversion to the piano lessons that Nora had insisted all her children have.

She hadn't been looking for someone to share her life. Chris had been planted there in a sneaky maneuver by her boss and she'd fought it every step of the way. Until Friday night, when he hadn't been there to argue with. Or laugh with. She'd missed him. But she'd still been afraid to admit that he'd filled a space in her life she didn't even know was empty.

Until now.

* * *

"Don't take this the wrong way, but it's nice to have you home again."

Chris scowled at his twin as she flopped down into one of the leather armchairs in the library. "Just to bring you up to speed, pest, I'm Felicity's bodyguard. Where she is, I am."

"Well, I'm glad she's here, then," Heather said, a mischievous sparkle in her eyes. "It's like old times. Vera Mae scolding you for snitching a piece of cake. Tripping over your shoes in the front hallway. Watching you fall head over heels for a reporter…"

Heather's last statement reeled Chris in, just like she knew it would. "What?" His voice cracked and he realized he sounded like the boys on his basketball team.

"A few months ago, I probably wouldn't have noticed, but now that I know what it feels like, I can recognize someone else with the same symptoms."

"You make it sound like a virus," Chris muttered, feeling his face get warm. If his sister had noticed, had Felicity? He was afraid to dwell on that unnerving thought. He tried one last time to convince her. And maybe himself.

"It's my job to keep a close eye on her."

"I don't know Felicity very well but my sisterly in-tuition tells me that I think she's everything you need," Heather said candidly. "And I think you might be everything *she* needs, too."

Chris groaned. "Please don't tell me that I look at her the way Ethan looks at you."

Heather grinned at him. "Since I just uncovered your deep, dark secret, it's only fair that you know one of mine. Mom's going to be pulling out one of those extra chairs very soon."

It took Chris a split second to figure out what she was talking about. Then, he wrapped his arms around her in a bear hug that lifted her off the floor. She squealed and pounded on his back.

"Congrats, sis," he murmured as he set her down again. "Not that I think anyone is good enough for you, but Ethan comes close."

"I'll be sure to pass that on to him," Heather said with a chuckle. "Don't tell anyone, all right? We're going to wait until the family dinner on Sunday. So far you're the only one with privilege."

"The blackmail possibilities are endless," Chris mused, rubbing his chin.

"Do I have to remind you that you're an officer of the law?" Heather planted her hands on her hips, but she was smiling. "You can tell Felicity if you want to."

"You don't quit, do you?"

"In fact, you can tell her now if you want to. I think she's been out of your sight now for a whole ten minutes!"

Chris scowled but one look at the grandfather clock in the corner told him she was right.

Chris found her in his mother's favorite spot—the cobblestone patio in the backyard. She hadn't heard him approach and as he got closer, he saw that her eyes were closed and her lips were moving. She was praying.

He paused, hesitant to interrupt her moment of solitude. Especially knowing that she wasn't going to like what he was about to say. He'd called Jason, who still hadn't been able to trace the roses to a local florist, and he'd already decided the next step was to canvas the neighborhood to see if anyone had noticed the boy who'd delivered them. It was a long shot, but he'd found that sometimes those paid off. Until he solved this, Felicity's safety came first.

"Uh-oh." Felicity's eyes were open now and she was studying him. "That's a pretty serious expression, Officer Hamilton."

Considering they'd only met two weeks ago, it was downright scary how well she read him. He sat down in the wicker rocker and held out his hand. Without hesitation, she reached out and he dropped something into it.

"That bad, huh?" Felicity looked down at the three caramel candies in her palm.

"I want you to take a leave of absence from the *Dispatch* until we figure out who wrote that letter." There. He'd said it. And he waited for the explosion he knew would follow.

"I figured you were going to ask me to do that." Felicity smiled.

Smiled?

Chris blinked, wondering if the stress of the last twenty-four hours had done internal damage.

"I thought about taking some time off," she admitted. "But then I prayed about it."

Chris sucked in a breath, pretty certain he wasn't going to like what was coming next. "Felicity—"

"I decided to take your advice."

Had he missed something? "My advice?" he repeated cautiously.

"When we were having lunch at Betty's that day, you said that you do everything you can to stay safe but there was a point when fear had to bow to faith. Remember?"

He yanked that conversation out of his memory file and silently skimmed through it. He *had* said that…but what kind of twist was Felicity going to put on it?

"Now you have to trust *me,* Chris. I agreed to stay at your house because I know it isn't safe at my apartment. I'll do my assignments at the *Dispatch* but I'll use the buddy system. I'll hang out with you in the evenings. I'll do everything I can to stay safe. I'll even tell my co-workers what's been going on. But this is that point you told me about—when I can't let fear get in the way of what God called me to do. He called you to be a cop. He called me to be a reporter. So, I'm going to do my job and trust that He's in control of the outcome."

Her earnest speech shifted him off balance. Everything she'd said was true. He just wished he wasn't the one who'd put those thoughts in her head to begin with.

"So what do you say?" she asked, her eyes searching his.

What could he say? *I don't want anything to happen*

*to you, not because it might make the news and give
Hamilton Media some bad press or even because Dad
asked me to? But because I'm getting used to you being
in my life?* The reality squeezed the air out of his lungs
and made it difficult to see past her copper eyes. "I say
that from now on, I'm not to say anything that can and
will be used against me."

Felicity grinned. "Here." She dropped the candies
back in his hand. "I think you need these more than I do."

A few hours later, Chris wandered into the dining
room. Nora, Heather and Felicity had all gone to bed
and he'd decided to spend the night in his old room. Not
because he didn't trust the security system but because
he hadn't had Vera Mae's buttermilk biscuits and gravy
for breakfast in months.

*Uh-huh. If it makes you feel better, keep telling
yourself that.*

He squashed the pesky thought and traced the top
of the dining room table with his fingertip. It almost
stretched the length of the room and as long as he could
remember, his family had gathered there for dinner.
Even now that he and his sisters and brothers were
adults, the table brought them back together once a
month. It was where they laughed. Argued. Thanked
God for His blessings. No matter where God took them
on their separate journeys, this table had always connected them.

He didn't even have to close his eyes to imagine each
member of his family taking his or her place at the
table. There had been times over the last few years that

he'd wanted to politely wriggle out of having dinner with his family. Conversations tended to naturally lean toward Hamilton Media and only made him feel even more of an outsider than usual. But no matter how he'd felt, no matter what silent struggles, personality clashes or misunderstandings each of them had brought to the table, they'd still been together. Maybe that in and of itself was a blessing.

He touched the back of Melissa's chair, remembering the day she'd hidden her peas underneath her plate, creating a perfect squished green circle for Vera Mae to discover when she'd cleared the table. Her tendency to run from life's unpleasant realities had continued through her teen years and beyond. Case in point— Dean Orton.

Frustration shot through him. Lately no one in the family had asked him if he was making any progress in his search for Melissa. It should have taken some of the pressure off of him, but somehow it only made it worse. As if they'd resigned themselves to the fact that he couldn't fix the situation.

"Who sits there?" Felicity's soft voice intruded on his thoughts but didn't do anything to relax the knots that had taken up residence inside of him. In fact, her unexpected presence had just the opposite effect!

"Melissa." He couldn't look at her. Not when it felt like every emotion was right there in his eyes for her to see.

"This is the biggest table I've ever seen." Felicity came into the room and stood beside him. He didn't have to look at her to know she was wearing comfortable sweats or that her hair was unconfined, skimming over her slim shoulders and down her back. All he'd done was glance at her when he'd heard her voice and everything about her had been instantly imprinted in his mind. And he couldn't credit any of his training for it, either. Felicity just seemed to have that effect on him.

"Mom likes to plan ahead. She bought this table when she and Dad were first married because she always wanted a big family and lots of noise. She got both. When Jeremy was eighteen, she started buying more chairs. One here, one there. Even though they're strategically placed in various rooms around the house, we all know what they're really for." Chris shook his head at Felicity's blank look. "Significant others. Spouses. She can't wait to add another six chairs to the table."

"I see." Felicity smiled. "Moms are like that. I think my mom's given up on me, though, so my sisters get most of the hints."

"Moms never give up on seeing their children happily married," Chris felt the need to point out. "Amy is thirty and Mom knitted her a blanket last year with a bunny in the corner. It didn't exactly match her decor, if you know what I mean."

As affection warmed Chris's voice, Felicity sensed his tension ease. When she'd seen him from the doorway, standing in the dining room and gripping the back of one of the chairs, she'd sensed his inner turmoil. And she had a pretty good idea what was causing it. She'd spent the better part of the evening listening to Heather relay stories from their childhood and it hadn't taken Felicity long to realize that Chris had always viewed himself as a weird offshoot in the family tree.

She had a feeling that Wallace Hamilton was to blame for some of that. Nora, however, radiated a mother's love and pride for her offspring and it was evident in every glance she'd bestowed on Chris that evening.

They'd shared an informal meal on the patio earlier as Nora gave them details about Wallace's condition. There had been times during the conversation when Nora had encouraged Heather and Chris and other times when she'd looked to them for strength. Her respect for Chris's mother had grown. Here was a woman who had somehow found the balance between needing and being needed. And Chris loved her. Maybe he'd been right when he'd bluntly told her that only weak men were intimidated by strong women....

"I better get to sleep." Felicity took a step toward the door. Call her a coward but she wasn't going to let her thoughts go down that slippery slope.

"I thought you *were* asleep. I should have known better." Chris leaned against one of the chairs and smiled down at her, blessedly unaware of the rollercoaster ride her thoughts were taking.

"I was working on my feature," Felicity said, distracted by his lazy smile—the one that seemed a bit more potent in the low light of the dining room. "It's taken me over a month to do the research and get the interviews I need. Wes Greene has been holding out on me but I'll have an interview by the end of the week if it kills me." Especially now that she'd seen those blueprints.

"Wes Greene?" Chris's smile faded. "What does he have to do with the story you're working on?"

"Since the feature is about the debate over what constitutes community development, I wanted to get his perspective. He's a developer—"

"Who doesn't blink at bending the law to get what he wants."

Felicity's heart jumped. "Do you know that for sure?"

"If I could prove it, he'd be in jail instead of buying everything he can get his hands on," Chris said. "If there's room on a piece of land for an expensive condo or a new mall, he's right there with his lawyer and a checkbook."

One by one, several puzzle pieces clicked into place. Wes Greene's lawyer at City Hall. River Street property suddenly being taken off the market, including the three buildings that Youth Connections had wanted to purchase. The mayor denying he'd known about a proposed domestic-abuse shelter on River Street. And the threatening letters that had arrived shortly after she'd started interviewing people for her feature.

She swallowed hard against the sudden churning in

her stomach. Maybe she and Chris had been wrong all along. Maybe she hadn't become a target because of an article she'd already written.

Maybe it was the one she hadn't finished yet.

Chapter Seventeen

"Have you seen this?" Tim strode into the back room of the P.D. and dropped a newspaper on the desk in front of Chris.

Chris found himself looking at the front page of the latest issue of the *Observer.*

Dispatch Reporter Harassed By Stalker

The story went on to mention Felicity by name and also gave a detailed account of the threatening letters she'd received, her slashed tires and the anonymous bouquet of dead flowers she'd had delivered to her apartment over the weekend.

"It wasn't enough that someone leaked this to the *Observer* but at the end of the article they felt it necessary to remind everyone that Jeremy isn't Dad's son and he's no longer in charge of Hamilton Media," Tim went on. "What's next? Publishing Dad's medical records?"

Chris could understand his brother's anger. Even

though the two newspapers were rivals, the *Observer* had never waged such a personal attack against his family.

"I dropped Felicity off at work this morning but I'm not sure if she's seen this yet," Chris said slowly.

"Oh, I'm sure she's seen it. the *Observer* probably hand-delivered a copy to her," Tim said bitterly. "Is it possible that the stalker leaked the information? The slashed tires—no one else knew about that, did they? And what about the flowers? I thought you were keeping this investigation quiet. No one should have known about those things."

Chris silently cautioned himself that Tim wasn't upset with him but at the situation. And he couldn't fault his brother for voicing the same questions that were hammering at him. Which showed that he and Tim were thinking along the same lines. A whole new phenomenon. "Only Jason and Captain Driscoll knew about the tires and the flowers. In fact, I was just leaving to interview Felicity's neighbors to see if anyone could identify the delivery person."

"I'm going to call the *Observer*'s editor and get to the bottom of this," Tim growled. "Once I get a name, you can do the cop thing and check it out."

In spite of the seriousness of the situation, Chris's lips twitched. The cop thing. That was an interesting twist on his chosen career.

A complimentary issue of the *Observer* had been on Felicity's desk when she got to work, the bold headline and story baring her private life for everyone to see. But that wasn't the reason why she'd barely made her morning deadline.

Resolutely she'd put the newspaper aside as she tried to find a connection between RiverMill Developers and the property on River Street. Even though Chris had told her that Mr. Sykes, the owner of the buildings that Youth Connections wanted to buy, had simply explained he'd decided not to sell at this point, Felicity wanted to talk to him again. Maybe Sykes had been offered more money—or been bullied into taking the property off the market.

If Wes Greene was as motivated as Chris said he was, anything was possible. What she couldn't understand was if RiverMill Developers did want the property, why be so secretive about it? Why not just put an offer on the table? And who was their connection at City Hall?

Felicity scribbled the names of the city councilmen on a sheet of paper and studied them. Then she added Mayor Whitmore and Ernest Cromwell to the mix. Every one of those people would have been present at the meetings she covered for the *Dispatch*. Any one of them could have found out about the feature she was writing and decided that she might stumble onto the truth before the sale went through.

Which might be the answer to one of her questions. At the center of the political debate over community development was tax dollars. If RiverMill stripped away three-quarters of the old buildings on River Street, it would displace a group of unemployed factory workers and lower-income families. The controversy over that decision would divide the city into two camps—the people who would say "good riddance" and those who wanted to "take care of their own."

Mayor Whitmore had always put himself firmly in the category of the latter, but Felicity wasn't sure about him anymore. She'd been a reporter long enough to know that sometimes people in power said one thing while their actions said the opposite. The mayor would have a lot of explaining to do if he had anything to do with Wes Greene buying River Street property.

And somehow she'd gotten caught in the middle.

If her hunch was right, the stalker had started his attack by writing the letters to the editor, maybe hoping that she'd be reassigned. When that didn't happen, he turned his attention to threatening her. A woman alone would be vulnerable. Maybe feel frightened enough to quit the newspaper and go back to California.

Except she wasn't alone. Felicity's gaze drifted from her notes and she reached out to touch the satin-soft petals of the flowers that had been delivered shortly after she'd arrived at work that morning. This time they weren't roses but a fragrant tangle of daisies and carnations in an array of confetti-bright hues.

The card wasn't signed but it didn't have to be. She knew Chris had sent them. She wasn't sure whether he'd sent them to strip away the image of the dead roses or to cheer her up after finding out that she was going to be this week's gossip, but it didn't matter. He'd sent them. Which put a whole new spin on the conclusion she'd drawn that to Chris, she was just "business as usual." Ever the professional, she doubted that Chris made a habit of sending flowers to the citizens of Davis Landing!

She closed her eyes and breathed in the sweet scent, wondering if she should have told Chris about her suspicions the night before. Sometimes puzzle pieces looked like they should fit but there was the tiniest gap between them. Then you had to start the search all over again. Felicity wanted to be sure that there weren't any gaps. There were peoples' reputations at stake and she wasn't going to present Ed or Tim with a scrambled bunch of notes and question marks. That's what Perry Sharpe did at the *Observer.* It sold papers, but did nothing for the integrity of the newspaper.

Felicity took a deep breath.

Okay, Lord, You were with Joshua when You told him to march around the walls of Jericho. Help me bring down some walls here, too. Show me who's on the other side.

"Felicity Simmons. *Dispatch.*" Felicity picked up her phone on the first ring. She'd been waiting all afternoon to see if the irritating number of calls she'd directed to Wes Greene's office were finally going to pay off.

"Miss, ah, Simmons." The male voice on the other line wasn't one she recognized. "I understand you're looking for information."

Felicity exhaled silently. "Who is this?"

"Not yet," he said, his voice cracking nervously. "I want to meet you somewhere, though. There's a diner near Nashville. A truck stop." He rattled off some directions and Felicity quickly jotted them down. "Can you meet me there now?"

"I'll be there as soon as I can."

There was a pause. "You can't tell anyone. I mean it, Miss Simmons. You'll get me in a lot of trouble if you do."

Felicity chewed on her lower lip. Chris was such a familiar face in the community, if her source saw him anywhere near her, the interview would end before it began.

Maybe she was talking to Roland Sykes. He'd proved to be just as elusive as Wes Greene. Felicity took a deep breath. There was only one way to find out.

Chris's shift was officially about to end when the secretary tracked him down.

"There's a woman here to see you. A Mrs. Mitowski. Apparently she was visiting her son for a few days and just found out from one of the neighbors that you were asking questions about a delivery boy?"

Chris's mouth went dry. Without a word he turned on his heel and went straight to the interview room, where an elderly woman had settled into a chair to wait for him.

"Mrs. Mitowski, I'm Officer Hamilton. The secretary said you might have some information about a teenager who delivered some flowers to an apartment near your home on Saturday," Chris said, easing the conversation into the direction he wanted it to go.

"There's no might about it. I saw him with my own two eyes," Mrs. Mitowski said, swatting the arm of the chair for emphasis.

"Could you describe him for me?"

"About my grandson's age. Sixteen or seventeen. Tall and kind of skinny. Had hair that was two different colors. You know the type."

He did. He shot hoops with them every week. The description was vague but Chris jotted it down. "Did you happen to notice what kind of vehicle he was driving?"

"Something red with a very loud muffler."

"You didn't happen to get a license plate number?" He asked the question automatically and was stunned when Mrs. Mitowski nodded vigorously.

"Yes, I did. I remembered it because it was one of those personalized plates. It said ZMANN."

Chris felt a rush of adrenaline. This was better than a physical description of the suspect. A license plate would bring Chris right to his front door.

"Oh, man. It wasn't me." A lanky kid fitting Mrs. Mitowski's description took one look at Jason and Chris standing outside the door and started to close it in their faces.

"Whoa, wait a second. We just want to talk to you, Zach." Jason stuck the toe of his boot in the door before it closed completely.

"If this is about the graffiti—"

"No graffiti," Chris said. "It's about the flowers you delivered last Saturday."

"Aw, that was just a favor for a friend." Zach visibly relaxed and Chris took advantage of the moment.

"So you won't mind answering a few questions."

"Come on in." He shrugged. "Sorry about the mess. The maid's on vacation."

"Bummer," Jason said dryly.

Zach slumped into a tweed recliner that listed slightly to one side. "So whaddaya wanna know?"

"Who asked you to deliver the flowers?"

"Mickey Howe. He was supposed to but he and his girlfriend got in a fight, so he called me and asked me to do it. Paid me ten bucks. Didn't seem like a big deal. The chick complain about them or something?"

"Or something," Chris said. "Do you know who hired him?"

"Naw." Zach's expression shut down and he scratched the three whiskers under his chin, his eyes shifting away from them.

"Graffiti," Jason said suddenly. "That wouldn't have been the bridge last Friday night, would it? I think someone turned in a home video on that one…."

Zach's Adam's apple suddenly leaped against his throat. "I've got Mickey's number in my cell."

"Call him," Chris said, keenly aware that Felicity was waiting for him at the *Dispatch*.

Zach pulled a high-tech phone out of the pocket of his ragged jeans and, with a wary eye on the two police officers, dialed his friend's number. "Sorry, he's not picking up."

"Where does Mickey work?" Chris asked. If the kid said RiverMill Developers...

"He does all kinds of stuff. He works at the Burger Bin on the weekends and he's a courier at the courthouse. Gets to ride a really cool bike...."

Chris's gut clenched and he headed toward the door.

Jason was right behind him. "What do you want me to do?"

"Get Mayor Whitmore on the phone."

He punched in Felicity's number on his phone but was immediately diverted to her voice mail. Both Tim's office and personal lines were busy and Chris struggled to check his frustration.

"Everything okay?" Jason asked, slanting a look at him as they headed toward City Hall.

Chris wasn't sure how to respond. The information Zach had given them could be the break they were looking for, but that didn't stop an uneasy feeling from snaking through him.

Lord, help me solve this. I know You always shine your light in the darkness and reveal the truth. But please—watch out for Felicity.

One look at the diner as she pulled into the parking lot and Felicity guessed its reputation must have been posted on Web sites around Tennessee, which was probably why the parking lot was almost empty during the dinner hour.

So much for the security of meeting in a public place.

Which was the only reason why Tim had finally agreed to let her go alone to meet with the man who'd called. She'd kept her promise to Chris and sought Tim out before she'd left, but if he'd seen her destination he probably would have blocked the door and taken her car keys away. Or volunteered to go with her. He'd insisted she wait for Chris, but boss or not, she'd refused. The voice on the phone had been shaky, stressed. If it was Sykes and she was late meeting him, he might not hang around and wait for her. She couldn't risk losing the chance to put the final pieces of the puzzle together.

Breathing a silent prayer for courage, Felicity walked into the diner and was relieved to see there were actually people inside. Several men were hunched together in a booth, their attention riveted on the grainy television set on the wall. The waitress, wearing a grease-spattered uniform, barely glanced her way as she wiped down one of the booths.

"Miss Simmons. Glad you could join me."

The familiar voice came from behind her and a chill shot up Felicity's back, tripping her heart into an uneven beat.

"Ernest." She turned slowly, unwilling to let the mayor's aide see the fear in her eyes.

"You were hoping for Mr. Sykes?" Ernest Cromwell asked, his lips twisting into a parody of a smile. "You did want to meet Sykes, didn't you? Or was it Wes Greene? I can't keep track. You've been such a busy girl this week."

Chapter Eighteen

"Not as busy as you've been," Felicity muttered.

Ernest's hand snaked out and caught her wrist. "That's your fault. You're not the only one with ambition. Your little story would have sunk my career."

"River Street." She'd thought Mayor Whitmore was the one who was behind the property sale. Not for a second had she suspected it might be Ernest.

"Let's talk somewhere where we can have a little more privacy, shall we?" Ernest gave her wrist a subtle squeeze.

Felicity looked for the waitress but she'd disappeared into the kitchen. The men in the booth weren't paying any attention to them. Still, she balked, hoping they'd glance her way and realize something was wrong.

Ernest laughed softly. "Don't bother. Why do you think I picked this place? Every one of those guys probably has a felony warrant on them. They're not about to dial 911. Come on."

They walked outside to the parking lot and Felicity's mind began to race. What had Chris told her about a stalker like Ernest? He blamed her for something? Wanted to get even?

Your little story would have sunk my career.

"Is Mayor Whitmore involved in this?"

"Are you taking notes for your replacement?" Ernest sneered. "Whitmore can't see the big picture. He'd rather let those losers living off state aid take up space on a prime piece of river property than get the tax dollars from Greene's pricey condos. Stupid. When I run for mayor, things are going to change."

Ernest and reality had parted company, Felicity decided. She wondered if there was a shred of logic left in the man's head. Only one way to find out. "So you want me to back off, is that it?"

"It's too late for that." Ernest's sudden frown questioned whether she was as smart as he thought she was. "If this gets out, it's over. *I'm* over. It isn't healthy for a man to disappoint someone like Greene. If I do, I'll lose his support when I run for mayor and a nice fat finder's fee for presenting him with the River Street property. No one will know I had anything to do with it. People are going to assume, just like you did, that Whitmore has been lying to them. He may even get to retire earlier than he planned."

Okay, she'd wanted the pieces of the puzzle and now she had them. Every psycho-shaped one of them.

"Ernest—"

"You don't mind if I drive, do you?" Ernest held out

his hand for the keys. "I always loved this car. The new tires look great, too."

At the reminder, Felicity's anger began to catch up to her fear. Tim knew where she was. Maybe by now Chris did, too. If she could just stall Ernest…

"People are going to look for me."

"They won't when you call your cop friend and your boss and tell them you're scared and you decided to go back to sunny California. No one will look for you…for a while." He tilted his head, considering his own words. Then he shrugged. "It's too bad you didn't take the hint when you got my letters. But don't worry, you'll make the front page, just not the way you'd hoped. You have to learn to be flexible, my dear."

Chris pressed the accelerator to the floor of the squad car, pushing the speed limit. Technically he was out of his jurisdiction but Jason had radioed the Nashville P.D., who promised to send an officer to the diner.

His heart had almost stopped beating when the dispatcher, who'd gotten busy with a 911 call, finally radioed and told him that Tim had been trying to reach him. She'd erroneously assumed it was simply a family matter that could wait until Chris was free. Sick to his stomach, all he could do was pray that he'd find Felicity safe and sound.

Ernest Cromwell. The mayor's aide.

He still couldn't believe it was Cromwell they'd discovered crouching in the shadows. The mayor had willingly cooperated and tracked down Mickey, who'd told them it had been Ernest who'd hired him to deliver the flowers to "a special lady."

It gave Chris the creeps just thinking about Ernest describing Felicity that way. How far was Cromwell willing to go to cover up his involvement in Felicity's case?

Lord, Felicity trusts that You're going to take care of her. Protect her.

You need to trust me, too.

The quiet thought reflected off his frantic appeal and he took a deep breath as he let it sink in. Maybe it was time to take the advice he'd so easily given to Felicity. Let fear bow to faith. That was fine when he was talking about himself and his career but it didn't always work so well when it came to the people he loved. Melissa. Jeremy. His father.

Felicity.

Ultimately, God was in control, not him. As hard as that was to get his mind around sometimes.

Lord, forgive me for not trusting You. For thinking it's always my responsibility to protect everyone in my life. Whatever happens, I do trust You.

And that's when Felicity's blue Caddie breezed past him.

Felicity couldn't hear much of anything but the rush of the highway from where she was. Which happened to be the trunk of her Caddie. Ernest had been savvy enough to take her cell phone and anything she could use as a pick to open the trunk. Maybe under different circumstances she would have taken it as a compliment to be described as "annoyingly resourceful."

She'd balked when Ernest had driven around to the back of the diner and demanded that she get in the trunk, but complied when she realized every breath she was able to take gave Chris more time to find her. Alive.

The verse from Joshua was like the comfort of a lullaby as her Cadillac sped along. Maybe the car hadn't simply been a gift from her frugal grandfather; maybe its purpose had always been to be a divine marker. She couldn't go half a block without someone staring at it, noticing it. Ernest hadn't thought about that. Stress was making him sloppy. Felicity prayed that it would get him caught.

When the car slowed down and stopped, Felicity wondered if they were at a traffic light and if she should start to make her presence known. Then she heard the sound of muffled voices. Slipping off one shoe, she began to bang it against the trunk.

Seconds later, the trunk popped opened and Chris was reaching for her. With his arms around her, Felicity took a gulp of fresh air, unable to speak.

"I don't know, Scoop," Chris murmured, tipping her chin so she was looking directly into his eyes. "This guy claims you sold him your Caddie. Did he know he wasn't going to have much trunk space?"

Felicity gave him a wobbly smile, eyeing Ernest, who was already handcuffed and glaring at them from the back seat of the squad car. "You knew it was him?"

"I think we both found out at the same time," Chris

said, brushing his thumb against a hot tear that rolled
down her cheek.

She hadn't realized she was crying.

"Go figure." Felicity exhaled raggedly.

"Let's get you home." As if he couldn't help himself,
Chris pulled her closer, closing his eyes briefly and
silently thanking God that she was safe. When he
opened them, he saw the expression in her eyes and
found himself thanking God all over again. "I'm glad
this is over. You really go all out to get a story. You
know, it's tough being your bodyguard, Felicity Simmons."

"Does this mean you're going to quit?" Felicity
allowed her disappointment to show.

"I'm willing to be reassigned." Then he kissed her.

"You call this news?" Wallace shook the latest issue
of the *Dispatch* at Chris, where the front-page headline
about Ernest Cromwell had Felicity's byline right
below it. She'd stayed up all night writing it and cheerfully presented it to Tim the next morning, then pro-
ceeded to take Chris's advice and put in for a short
leave of absence, which she planned to spend the
majority of napping on Nora's sunny patio.

She did manage to snag one more interview before
she left. Wes Greene had called to state for the record
that everything he'd done was "perfectly ethical and
legal." He had no idea that Ernest Cromwell had been
stalking Felicity or bribing River Street property
owners like Mr. Sykes into selling to RiverMill De-

velopers. Since there was no way to prove otherwise, they had to let him go. For now.

"At least you scooped the *Observer*," Wallace groused. "That's probably got them in a tizzy."

"What's wrong with the article, Dad?" Chris said carefully.

"It's totally objective!" Wallace said.

Chris glanced at Felicity, who was sitting in the chair near Wallace's bed. She wasn't at all intimidated by the great Wallace Hamilton and it showed in the cheeky wink she gave him.

"I thought newspapers were supposed to be objective."

"It doesn't mention a single thing about you rescuing the girl. Most of it's about that criminal Cromwell."

Chris tried not to smile. "I was just doing my job. It's not about getting my name in the paper or a plaque on the wall."

"Just doing your job?" Felicity muttered. "And here I tried to convince myself that I was special."

Chris reached out and took her hand, then brought it to his lips and kissed her knuckles. Wallace coughed and looked away, but there was the shadow of a smile on his face.

"It's a good story, Simmons. I mean Felicity," Wallace said grudgingly. Then he reached out and patted Chris's shoulder. "Maybe I'll just have to write my own article."

The pride he heard in his father's voice made

Chris's eyes sting and Felicity squeezed his fingers in understanding.

"And you, young lady, I suppose you want a raise."

Felicity was brave enough to lean over and plant a kiss on Wallace's hollow cheek. "Of course."

"We have to go, Dad. Felicity is moving back into her apartment this afternoon and I have a fish to transport."

"I kind of like Friday nights now," Felicity said as they walked to the parking lot.

"Why is that?" Chris played along.

"Someone to watch a video with."

"You picked out a video?"

Felicity nodded, her brown eyes full of innocence. "Sword fighting. Pirate ships. Danger. Cannons."

"It's a musical, isn't it?"

"The pirates may sing. Yes, I think they do."

Chris held out his hand. And Felicity dropped a caramel candy into it.

Epilogue

"**E**arth to Chris. Come in, Chris."

At Heather's soft whisper, Chris snapped to attention and realized everyone at the table was looking at him. There was a soft ripple of laughter and then Nora took pity on him.

"Stop teasing your brother," she said sternly, though her eyes sparkled with humor.

"But life would be so boring," Heather said irrepressibly.

"Are you sure you want to deal with this, Ethan?" Chris asked darkly. "I have a scar on my forehead that says she's a handful."

Heather gasped and her family members burst out laughing. Heather's sweet personality was acknowledged and appreciated by everyone she came in contact with. Especially her family.

"I'm looking forward to *dealing* with her, as you put

it," Ethan said, his gaze skimming Heather's pretty face. "In fact, I'd like to make it permanent."

Nora was the first one to understand his meaning. She jumped up from her chair and hurried to the other side of the table, catching both of them in a hug. "You're engaged!"

Tim lifted his glass of iced tea. "Smooth, Danes. Very smooth."

Ethan lifted Heather's hand and for the first time they noticed the beautiful diamond solitaire on her finger.

"It's beautiful," Amy said, catching her lower lip in her teeth. "Really, Heather. It's perfect for you."

"*Ethan* is perfect for me," Heather corrected her sister.

Chris thumped Ethan on the back. "You'll do, Ethan. There is a chair somewhere in this house with your name on it, you know."

"Chris!" Nora gave him an exasperated glance.

He was saved by his cell phone. Felicity's number was on the tiny screen and he stood up so quickly his own chair almost tipped over.

"We know who that is," Tim murmured.

Amy watched as Chris ducked out of the room to talk to Felicity.

"Would that be so bad?" Nora asked.

Ethan and Heather didn't respond to her question. They'd tuned everyone else out and Amy felt a stab of loss. Things were changing. Melissa and Jeremy were still gone. Wallace was still in the hospital. Her little sister was engaged. And Chris was showing all the signs of a man in love.

"It's a good thing we're not dominoes or all the rest of us would fall," Tim joked. "We don't want that."

"No," Amy said faintly. "We don't want that."

Maybe if she kept saying it, she'd convince herself.

Amy Hamilton is reunited with an
old boyfriend in THE FAMILY MAN,
by Irene Hannon; coming out September 2006,
only from Steeple Hill Love Inspired.
Please turn the page for a sneak peek.

The staff meeting had gone well. Amy had let Heather introduce Bryan Healey, and as the group tossed around story ideas for upcoming issues, he'd jumped right in, impressing her with his suggestions. He'd always had good instincts, and it was clear that time hadn't changed that. If anything, they'd been honed through the years, seasoned with experience and polished with practice. She'd particularly liked his idea about a story on separation anxiety—in *parents*. It was a unique twist on a familiar topic, and with his only son starting kindergarten in two days, he could write with authority on the subject.

As the meeting wound down, Amy stood. "I think that wraps things up, unless there are any other issues we need to discuss?" When no one spoke, she reached for her notepad. "Okay. The pizza should be here any minute, so don't wander too far. Although I don't think I've ever had to twist anyone's arm to take advantage of a free meal."

Her command elicited some chuckles, and as everyone gathered up their papers and rose, Amy turned to

Heather. "Would you check with Herman? The pizza should have been delivered by now."

"No problem."

This was the part of the meeting Amy had been dreading. After typical sessions, the staff just dispersed. But she had started a practice of welcoming new employees with a casual lunch after their first staff meeting. If Amy skipped the custom this time, it would raise questions—which she didn't need or want. Better to act as if this was any other welcome party. Meaning she had to stick around, mingle and chat with the new employee. The thing to do was talk business, she counseled herself. Stay away from personal topics.

Steeling herself, she walked over to the tub of soft drinks on a side table and chose a diet soda. Out of the corner of her eye, she noted that Bryan was talking with a couple of other writers in the far corner. Good. As long as they kept him occupied, she could lay low. And once the pizza arrived, she'd grab a piece, say a few words to Bryan and disappear.

"Pizza's here!" Heather called from the doorway hauling several large flat boxes. As she spread them out on the conference table, the staff converged like hungry buzzards. All except Bryan, Amy realized. He was still standing off to the side, one shoulder propped against the wall, his hands in the pockets of his khaki slacks. As if sensing her perusal, he angled his head in her direction and looked at her. Short of being rude, she saw little option but to join him. Better to get it over with, anyway.

As she walked toward him, he straightened up. With her heels adding three inches to her five-foot-five stature, Amy was only two or three inches shorter than Bryan. As a result, she didn't have to look up very far to get a good view into his deep green eyes. Though cool and dispassionate now, Amy recalled with a pang how they had once radiated warmth and devotion. The contrast produced an almost physical ache in her heart. One she didn't intend to dwell on. It was obvious that Bryan had gotten over her long ago. And she had no one to blame for that except herself.

In retrospect, she knew that her cavalier assumption that he would wait around until she was ready to make a commitment had been arrogant and insensitive. She'd known how much family meant to him. Known how much he wanted to establish a home of his own. But she'd disregarded his needs, his aspirations. Maybe if they'd talked they could have found a compromise. Instead, Amy had expected him to dance to her music. Even when he'd stopped calling, she'd just assumed he was giving her the space she'd asked for. His profession of love had been so ardent, so sincere, that it had never occurred to her that he was giving his heart to someone else. By the time she'd realized what she'd lost, it had been too late. He'd been committed to another, and pride had kept her from contacting him. End of story. Or so she'd thought—until his résumé crossed her desk. Now he was back, stirring up embers of the flame that had once burned in her heart for him. And she had no idea how to deal with it.

She stopped beside him and tried for a smile, hoping that her inner turmoil wasn't reflected on her face. "So…did you find the meeting helpful?" Her tone was a little too bright, and the speculative look on his face told her that he'd noticed.

"It was a good chance to get a feel for everyone's working style. I'm glad you came over. I wanted to thank you for offering me the job."

"It was Heather's decision."

"But not without your stamp of approval, I'm sure."

Since she couldn't refute that, she remained silent.

Glancing over her shoulder, he lowered his voice. "I hope this isn't too awkward for you."

Jolted by his direct approach, Amy stared at him. But she supposed she shouldn't be surprised. Bryan never had been one to dance around issues. Put the problem on the table, deal with it and move on. That had always been his philosophy. And still was, it seemed.

"No." She carefully lifted one shoulder in an indifferent shrug. "Our history is…ancient. A lot of things have happened since then. And we've both moved on with our lives."

"True." His gaze flickered to her ringless left hand, which had a death grip on the notebook she was clutching to her chest. "I hear you've never married."

His unexpected comment threw her for a second, but she made a quick recovery. "No time. Work has been pretty all-consuming."

A sardonic smile touched the corners of his mouth. "You always did have more important things to do."

That hurt. Especially since he was right. Back in her school days, when she'd planned to take the publishing world by storm, the only thing on her radar screen had been her career. But her priorities were different now, even if Bryan had no way of knowing that. Or of knowing that her workaholic style was an escape from loneliness, not an end in itself.

* * * * *

Dear Reader,

It was a blessing to be included in the DAVIS LANDING
continuity series, I hope you enjoy getting to know the
entire Hamilton family! Chris and Felicity, the hero and
heroine of *By Her Side,* are particularly close to my
heart. Both are believers, but God provides an avenue for
growth during a stressful time in their lives—something
He does with all of us if we allow it. As I wrote this
book, a verse in Galatians kept coming to mind: "Carry
each other's burdens, and in this way you will fulfill
the law of Christ." Whether it was Felicity learning that
God sometimes offers His strength in the form of other
believers or the Hamilton family leaning on each other
during Wallace's illness, it is important that we not walk
independently of one another. One of the best gifts God
has given to us is each other!

I love to hear from my readers. If this book has touched
you in any way, please let me know. You can contact me
at my Web site, www.loveinspiredauthors.com.

Blessings,

Kathryn Springer

QUESTIONS FOR DISCUSSION

1. Both Felicity and Chris came from close-knit families. In what ways do you think their upbringing may have been similar? In what ways do you think it might have been different?

2. What strengths did you see in Felicity that helped her succeed as a reporter? What about in Chris as a police officer? In what areas did their independent personalities complement each other and in what ways did they clash?

3. When she was a child Felicity had an unsettling experience that affected her faith. What was the core issue for her? How did Chris acting as her bodyguard begin to bring that issue back to the surface, and did she handle it the right way?

4. Chris is a believer but he still had a major struggle in what area of his life? How did this carry into his relationship with Felicity? With his family? With God?

5. Felicity's dad came up with a creative way for Felicity to deal with her anger when she was a child. Did your parents (or do you) have a favorite scripture, quote or other method you use to develop healthy ways to deal with emotions? What is it?

6. How does Felicity's perception of herself change by the end of the book?

7. Chris has always felt like an outsider because he chose to be a police officer instead of joining the family business. Do you think his perception was accurate? Based on what?

8. At what point in the story did you begin to piece together who the stalker might be? What were the clues that brought you to that conclusion?

9. In what ways did Chris bring some balance back into Felicity's life?

10. What is your favorite scene in the book? Why?

2 Love Inspired novels and a mystery gift... Absolutely FREE!

Visit

www.LoveInspiredBooks.com

for your two FREE books, sent directly to you!

BONUS: Choose between regular print or our NEW larger print format!

There's no catch! You're under no obligation to buy anything. We charge nothing—ZERO—for your first shipment. And you don't have to make any minimum number of purchases.

You'll like the convenience of home delivery at our special discount prices, and you'll love your free subscription to Steeple Hill News, our members-only newsletter.

We hope that after receiving your free books, you'll want to remain a subscriber. But the choice is yours—to continue or cancel, anytime at all! So why not take us up on our invitation, with no risk of any kind!

Love Inspired®

LIGEN05

Love Inspired®

A LOVE SO STRONG

BY

ARLENE JAMES

He'd prayed to God for
the perfect woman. What
pastor Marcus Wheeler
got was Nicole Archer.
While she was kind and
beautiful, Marcus Wheeler
thought she was too young
and unconventional to be a
proper pastor's wife.
Yet sometimes God's plan
isn't what one expects....

*Available September 2006
wherever you buy books.*

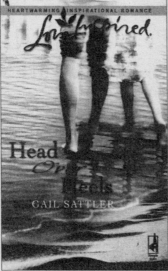

Love Inspired

No Place Like Home

BY

Debra Clopton

After getting stranded in Mule Hollow, candy maker Dottie Hart knew she wouldn't be able to help her brother with his women's shelter. Sheriff Brady Cannon was there to assist her, but the local matchmakers had another agenda— giving Dottie and Brady a happily-ever-after.

Available September 2006 wherever you buy books.

Steeple Hill®